MYSTERIES ON IONA FEATURING EVERYONE'S
FAVORITE BENEDICTINE SLEUTH
FATHER COLUMBA

GOOD FOR the SOUL

James T. Baker

Green Hills Press
Nashville

Good for the Soul

Green Hills Press
Nashville, Tennessee
www.greenhillspress.com
© 2013 James T. Baker

In Publication Data
1.Fiction 2. Mystery
ISBN: 978-0-9855342-1-9

Published with the services of Grave Distractions Publications. www.gravedistractions.com

Cover Design and Interior Layout: Brian Kannard; Grave Distractions Publications.

Father Columba is portrayed by John Kannard.

Background image of Fingal's Cave provided via Creative Commons License 3.0 license and was taken by Karl Gruber. For more information about Creative Commons, please visit www.creativecommons.org/licenses/by-sa/3.0/deed.en.

Rich & Hope

you enjoy this

don't Overlook

a few tips

... like

mixed.

James Dean

2016

I t all began the night I was summoned to the office of my Abbot, my Father Superior. Or maybe it began when he assigned me to be Novice Master for the Arch Abbey. Or maybe it began when I entered the Benedictine Order out of spite for the way God had treated me, taking away my father at too early an age, and I was hoping to foul up His plan to bring in the Kingdom. Anyway, I'll begin my story with the hour when I knocked at the Abbot's door, heard him bid me "come," and entered his sanctum sanctorum to hear what he had to tell me.

I had been back at Saint Vincent's for a year—this time. I had "retired" there in 1961, after teaching history at several Catholic colleges around the country for thirty years. Soon after arriving there, however, Father Superior had sent me to sort out some administrative problems at our mission Priory in Mississippi, where I was called upon to solve—of all things—a murder mystery. I was then 65 years old and retired from full time teaching. I thought I was entering my years of leisure and perhaps my dotage when I accepted that assignment, to clear up a minor mess, and found myself involved in a homicide. I have recorded that story in a diary, a rather plump one; it is in my lock box at the Arch Abbey, and maybe someday after all the people involved are dead I might send it to a publisher. Or I may die first.

Almost the moment I returned from Mississippi to Saint Vincent's, at age 66, Father Superior sent me to Korea, to one of our priories there, because of another mysterious death. I have the details of that debacle in another diary, not quite as plump as the first but also in my lock box. Once again a lot of people will have to die, on both sides of the Pacific, before I offer it for publication. As with the Mississippi adventure, I may die first.

I assumed, when I returned "home" from Korea in 1963, at age 67, that I would at last be allowed to retire completely and comfortably. Saint Vincent's operates a small liberal arts college and a seminary, and before I went off to Mississippi and then to Korea I had taught there part time: a history course now and then for the college, a catechism class now and then for the seminary. Now I assumed I would return to that routine, be put out to pasture, be allowed to vegetate. I would be able to keep busy enough, but I would never have to investigate another killing. So much for assumptions!

Right away after I got over the jet lag caused by flying from Korea to Japan to San Francisco to Philadelphia to La Trobe, Father Superior called me in and told me that the Novice Master, Father James, had died while I was away and that he wanted to put me in charge of training the new lads, to help prepare them for their lives as monks. As with all of his other commands, despite misgivings, I submitted to his will. I had never considered myself a good monk, and I doubted I could make the kids coming in good ones, but I had taken an oath of obedience, and I would do my best to be. . .obedient.

It was less than a year later, the early summer of 1964, and I was 68, when the Abbot called once more called me to his study and began the story I will now record. Father was smoking one of his menthol cigarettes, as he did from the time he woke in the morning until he fell asleep at night, except when he ate, which was rarely and sparingly, and when he said mass. Actually I have even seen him smoke between his soup and his sandwich, between his sandwich and his pudding. I have seen him hurry through the last few lines of a mass in order to duck out into the vestry for a puff. His conversation with me that night was punctuated, as always, with coughing, at times violent. I have often wondered how he held onto life for so many years when he was obviously trying to kill himself. He was thin and ashen, and every cough brought up phlegm; yet his eyes were sharp and piercing. He held himself erect and had not a doubt about any of the opinions he held or orders he gave—or that he would hold them and give the out them well into the future. Through a fog of smoke, he gestured for me to sit in the chair before his desk. As always, I obeyed.

Father Superior, once a missionary, had been a personal friend and confidant of Chinese President and Generalissimo Chiang Kai -shek during and just after World War II. They had traveled side by side during the conflict, they had celebrated V-J Day in Chiang's headquarters in the mountains outside Beijing, and for several years Father had translated crucial correspondence between Chiang and Roosevelt and then Chiang and Truman, from Mainland China and then from Taiwan, when the Communists sent Chiang running there. Now Father was in the process of establishing an institute at Saint Vincent's College to confer Ph.D. degrees on prominent members of Chiang's Nationalist Gwo-min-dong Party so that they could man the faculties of Taiwanese colleges being planted all over the island. Later this became something of a scandal when it was learned that the doctoral recipients spent less than a year in La Trobe and paid Benedictines to write their dissertations for them. In return for these favors, the Taiwanese government made generous gifts to the Arch Abbey and the school. Accrediting Boards do not look kindly on such arrangements.

Father Superior let me sit there in front of him for quite a long time before he spoke. This was probably intended to make me nervous, but it didn't because what did I have to fear? Sixty-eight and retired, I was oblivious to threats. When he realized I was not to be intimidated, he spoke.

"Columba. . .I will come directly to the point. I have had several complaints about you."

"Oh?" This was nothing new. People have been complaining about me all my life. Teachers, students, fellow monks, I always manage to rub someone in every group the wrong way. "Who is complaining and what about?" I asked as politely as I could manage, given the fact that although being criticized was not new, it was irritating. I felt my neck growing hot.

"Your novices. . ." He was suddenly attacked by a coughing fit, and it took him several agonizing seconds to fend it off and return to his sentence. ". . . your young men. . ."

"Yes?"

"And also members of your study group."

"My study group?"

Let me explain about my study group. In the early afternoon of November 22, 1963, I was lying in bed listening to my radio, to the classical music station in LaTrobe, when the news flash came from Dallas, Texas. I hurriedly got up and went down to the lounge, where some of the monks had turned on the television, and for six hours we all followed the events unfolding in Cow Town. At last, having missed supper in order to follow the drama, I returned to my room and let myself have the luxury of a good cry. Young John Kennedy was dead.

All that weekend I kept to myself, taking long walks down by the river, avoiding conversations with monks or students, noting how depressed the people I passed looked. John Fitzgerald Kennedy, our first Catholic president, was gone. So youthful, so eloquent, so promising; he was replaced by a man who looked and sounded like he had just fallen off a turnip truck. Johnson reminded me of characters I had known in Mississippi. The undergraduates, the seminarians, the monks, and the novices all walked around in a daze. Then after Sunday mass, as I was having the noon meal in the refectory, someone came in and told us to come to the television set again; and I watched as a reporter from Dallas recounted how the presumed assassin had himself been gunned down as he was being transferred from one police facility to another. I waited until the engineers could play a tape of the fiasco and watched as Oswald was taken out of a building and crouched in agony as a bullet penetrated his stomach. After an hour the reporter came back on and told us Oswald was dead.

Then came the funeral, the Boston Cardinal's flat nasal accent, the familiar Catholic rite, the veiled widow with the two remaining brothers, the little son saluting his father's casket, and for a week the College and the Arch Abbey mourned. From brief conversations with many of the men that week I got the impression that they had no idea how or why this had all happened. Both the monks and the students at St. Vincent's lived in a cocoon. They were isolated from the world outside our walls. It was then that I suggested to Father Abbot that I start a voluntary study group to discuss current events, the historical reasons they occurred, and particularly the ways we Catholics could apply our theology to the problems American society was facing. He readily agreed to my suggestion, and my study group was born.

I thought things had gone reasonably well. We started with just four members, two other retired monks and two seminarians; but within a few weeks there were eight of us, then twelve. Each week I brought up a pertinent issue, explained its historical background, and encouraged everyone to speak his mind. There were some lively disputations, yes, but no one had seemed upset by anything we said or did. That's why I was taken aback by Father Superior's announcement that he had received complaints.

"From the novices *and* from people in the study group?" I said, trying to take this in. What had I done?

"Yes. Two or three in each group. They are disturbed."

"What has them upset?" I asked. "In the novice class we are following the book of instructions you chose, page by page, item by item, covering everything needed to prepare them for solemn vows. In the discussion class, I can assure you that everyone has an equal opportunity to speak his mind."

"No, it's nothing like that. The novices agree that you are covering the material. Members of the study group like the choice of topics. It's. . .well. . .it's you, Columba. It's your views on certain things, particularly your views about the nature, the character of God. You are very articulate. If you were not, what you say would probably have less effect. It's why you have been a successful teacher all these years. You speak your mind. . .about God, about the Nature of God. . .so dramatically, so articulately. . .and you do it repeatedly, apparently in every discussion. . .that you frighten some of the men."

"I do? I frighten them? How?"

I was truly puzzled. What had I said? It's true that I have some strong opinions about God, "the Old Bastard" I call Him when He and I talk; and I suppose such language would offend some naïve persons; but I thought I had been circumspect. I thought I had kept my most caustic comments to myself. Maybe it was a sign of old age that I was spouting things in public that I thought I had kept private.

"Yes. They say that in every discussion you point out that the God of the Bible is demanding and merciless. They say they are concerned that you really do not believe in our Heavenly Father."

"That's not true, Joseph," I said. In my agitation I called him by his name, not his title. I didn't bother to correct the offense. "I have no doubts whatsoever about the existence of God. It's just that I don't like Him very much. He's not a nice old sugar daddy. I have had a running dispute with him all my life. He can at other times be terribly spiteful, even hateful. He took my father away from me when I was a boy. I've never forgiven Him for that."

"You mustn't say such things, Columba, even if you believe them. God didn't take away your father."

"No? Then who did? He's in charge of things. You see, my very animosity demonstrates how thoroughly I believe in God and in His omnipotence. I believe He is responsible for everything. And half of everything is bad; you know that as well as I do. The assassination for example."

"Yes," he nodded. He looked sad. We were all saddened by the events in Dallas. "I understand what you're saying, believe me I do. Sometimes it is hard to have faith in the goodness of Divine Providence. But he did not take away J.F.K. any more than he took away your dad."

"So you doubt He is really in charge. . ."

"I didn't say that."

"Personally I think He is still upset about the crucifixion, how we treated His

Son, and I think He gets a little measure of revenge on us at every opportunity."

"Columba. . ."

"No, I'm serious. J.F.K. is a prime example. God gave us this marvelous young man, a Roman Catholic president, and then He snatched him away from us. Remember the scripture: 'The Lord giveth, the Lord taketh away, blessed be the name of the Lord.' I agree with the first part but not the second. I don't agree with the person who says, 'Whatever God does is automatically good.' I don't think all He does is blessed."

Father Superior signed, nodded, and then flashed me a bitter grin. "Columba, you and I are educated men. We are, if I may be a bit arrogant, theologically sophisticated. We understand these things. We can discuss them without losing our faith. We can discuss the nature of God without doubting His existence. But you have to remember that the novices are young and naïve, and even some of the monks in your study group are simple brothers. They cannot deal with controversial theological principles. What you say hurts their faith. They are spreading the word that we are harboring a. . .heretic. You."

"Me? A heretic?" I sat up straight in my chair and leaned toward him. "Father, I am about as orthodox as you will find. I believe that Jesus is God's Son—but that He inherited only the good side of the Father's nature. He is without malice, filled with love. I think of Him as being very much like my Uncle Ed, who helped raise me after my father died. I believe that in the Eucharist the bread and wine become the body and blood of Christ. I pray to the Virgin Mary, who to my mind is very much like my sainted mother. I am obedient to a fault to the Holy Catholic Church, personified in this Abbey by you. So I ask you, how am I a heretic?" I sat back and waited for an answer.

Father Superior coughed, and he struggled to stop. It hurt me to listen to him gag that way. When he had recovered, he forced a pained smile and shook his head. "You're not a heretic, Columba, of course you're not. What you are is smart, you can live with contradictions, but the novices and these monks in your study group. . . your provocative opinions about God's bad side shock them."

I knew what he was going to say, and so I decided to beat him to it. "I guess I had better resign as Novice Master," I sighed. "And I will no longer attend the discussion group."

He nodded. "Thank you, Columba. Thank you for relieving me of the onerous duty of 'firing' you." He laughed, but when I didn't join him he grew serious. "I have asked Father Philip to take over as Novice Master; and we will discontinue the study group for now. Perhaps later, with another leader, we can take it up again."

So it had been decided even before he called me in. So things seem to work in the Most Holy and Catholic Church. As always, I nodded my acceptance of the decision. I moved to get up and go. I felt dizzy. I wondered if I had forgotten, as I did so often, to take my blood pressure pill that morning.

"More than that," Father Abbot said, gesturing for me to keep seated. "I have decided that I think it might be good for you and for the Community for you to take a break. I think you should get away for a time." He grinned. "Things seem to go smoother around here when you are. . .not here."

I hated to hear that. Still I was ready to obey. "Yes," I said. "You're probably right."

"So. . ." He slapped his knees and smiled. "I have arranged for you to go on a retreat—it's a dream really. I wish I could go."

"A retreat? Where?"

"Iona."

"Iona?" My mind spun, trying to recollect information stored somewhere deep in a corner of my mind. It was a Catholic college. . .somewhere."

"Not Iona College," Father said as if he could read my mind. "Iona. The Holy Isle."

I dug deeper into my store of information. "Oh. Iona. The island. Off the coast of Scotland. With an Abbey founded in the Sixth Century. "You want me to go to Iona?"

"Yes, Iona. Saint Columba and all that. Columba. You were given his name. Probably because you are Irish."

"Yes," I mused, "that's what my first Abbot told me when he named me."

It was all coming back now. Saint Columba had come from Ireland to the tiny island of Iona only a half mile off the coast of Scotland in the Sixth Century, and from there he had launched a missionary enterprise that converted much of Britain and reached even into the barbarian continent of Europe. He had made Iona a place of pilgrimage, and many kings of Scotland and even of

Norway were buried there. The Benedictines had taken it over after the Norman Conquest, they had built a stone Abbey for the monks and a convent for nuns; but the brothers and sisters were turned out and the buildings had been destroyed during the Protestant Reformation.

"Is there anything on Iona now?" I asked. "The pictures I recall seeing show the Abbey and Convent in ruins."

"Oh no, that's all changed. One of the wealthy lairds of Scotland spent tons of money restoring the Abbey at the beginning of this century, and Iona is once again a pilgrimage destination. It's no longer strictly Catholic, but an interdenominational fellowship holds retreats there, both for individuals and for groups. Everyone who goes there helps out with chores, joins in recreational, worship, and discussion programs, and has plenty of time to reflect."

"So you want me to go there, with a group of Baptists. . ."

"Yes, Baptists, Methodists, Episcopalians, Agnostics. . ."

"Agnostics?"

"Yes. There are no admission requirements. Everyone is just supposed to spend a lot of time in solitude, thinking about religious matters, and then share his or her ideas with everyone in discussion groups. Individuals can either participate in group worship or go to the chapel and pray silently. I thought if you had a chance to do this, to exchange views with other smart people, people outside our own Church, your opinions about God might change, at least a little bit. And not least it will give emotions here a chance to cool a bit." He smiled for a moment before starting to fight off another cough.

I was stunned. Father Abbot considered me a menace, and he was sending me into exile. I shook my head.

"You will leave next Saturday. Each week at the Iona Retreat Center begins on Monday. I have booked you for three of these weeks consecutively. The fellowship is connected to British Telecom, so you can call me, or I can call you at regular intervals to see how you are doing."

I nodded. "Yes, Father."

He stood and held out a hand to me. The effect of tobacco was evident in the skin of his hands. He was only in his early fifties, but his hand looked like a claw. I started to kiss it, but he said, "Just shake it, Columba. You and I have no rank. We are equals before God."

I shook his hand. "Before God," I repeated. "Your God or mine?"

"He's all the same, Columba," Father Abbot said. "God bless you."

So I stumbled out of his office, my legs shaking. Not only had I been relieved of my job as Novice Master, not only had I lost my discussion group, but I was being banished from the Arch Abbey, I was being sent on a journey to a far country to live with pagans, and I had no idea when I could return home or whether I would ever again be given useful work to do. The greatest fear of aging is that a man might one day be unneeded, useless, worthless.

Instead of going back to my cell, I took a long walk down across the meadow that led to the river. Of course, as was true of almost every evening, I had a talk with an old familiar Voice.

"So, you've screwed me again," I sighed.

"I'VE SCREWED YOU? WHAT DO YOU MEAN BY THAT? IT WAS YOUR BIG MOUTH THAT GOT YOU INTO THIS SCRAPE."

"Yes, but it was talking about You that did it."

"YOU DIDN'T HAVE TO BRING ME UP. YOU COULD HAVE LEFT ME OUT OF YOUR DISCUSSIONS."

"Not when we're talking about Theology. The T-H-E in that word is your name, after all. The subject is T-H-E, God, You."

"WELL THEN YOU COULD HAVE AT LEAST KEPT YOUR OPINIONS ABOUT ME TO YOURSELF."

"You mean I could have lied."

"NO, NOT LIED, JUST KEPT QUIET ON THE SUBJECT. THAT'S NOT LYING."

"It's a sin to hold back the truth. In my book that's being deceitful, and being deceitful is lying, and lying is a sin."

"MAYBE. BUT ALL SINS ARE NOT THE SAME. THE SIN OF LYING IS NOT AS BAD AS THE SIN OF BLASPHEMY."

"The kids and the monks say I'm a heretic. They didn't say I was a blasphemer."

"YOU'RE PROBABLY BOTH. BUT I STILL LOVE YOU, YOU OLD HERETIC."

"Who's calling who old?"

"HA! YOU'VE GOT ME THERE."

"So you love me, eh? Well you've got a funny way of showing it. I try to be honest, try not to lie, and I'm made to be the Judas Goat, sent off into the wilderness in order to restore peace and harmony to the Community, to purge St. Vincent's of its sin."

"I'LL TRY TO MAKE IT INTERESTING FOR YOU IN THE WILDERNESS."

"I'll bet you will."

II

Columba knocked and entered the cell of his monastic superior knowing what he faced. He had violated a strict rule, he had done so with full awareness of the seriousness of his transgression, and he thought he knew what Father Abbot was going to say to him.

It was to the best of his Abbey's computation the Year of Our Lord 562, and Columba was Master of Education for his monastery in the Irish Kingdom of Ulster. He had been a monk there for ten years, had received the highest evaluation marks from his teachers and his Father Abbot, and two years before had been appointed to teach the new monastic volunteers. He had taken his job seriously, as he had always taken responsibilities seriously; and he was well respected, loved even, by his students. It was his desire to give them the very best education possible that had led him to violate one of the rules and had now brought him before a disciplinary committee.

As he came through the low door—he was a tall man, taller than those for whom the door had been designed, and he had to stoop—he saw Father Abbot and two other monks, all three of advanced age, who composed the committee that dealt with rules violations. They wore, as did he, the plain wool robes of his monastery, and they were all, as was he, clean shaven both face and head. Each monk was given a weekly shave, at the time of his weekly bath, to prevent him from spending valuable time in the frivolous pastime of grooming.

Columba bowed to each man in order of his age and then stood before them while they sat and looked him over. The three men had already conferred on his case, and they had already made a decision, and the Father Abbot did the talking for the three. He cleared his throat before speaking, and it was obvious that the winter cold he had developed back in December still plagued him even now in early spring. Columba could hear the lingering gurgle of congestion.

"Father Columba," he said with a rasp, which led to a wet cough, "we are deeply concerned about some of your behavior. I think you know the behavior I mean, don't you?"

Columba nodded. "Yes, Father."

"You made a copy of the Book of Psalms lent to us by the Abbey of Kells."

"I did."

"You knew this was against the rules."

"I did."

"The Abbot at Kells gave explicit instructions that the Book was to be read but not copied; it was to be returned to him after the five months required to do the Reading."

"I know that, Father. I knew it from the start."

"We were to have a Psalm read each day during our evening meal, and after we had finished we were to return the book—*uncopied*."

"That was my understanding."

"The Abbot of Kells jealously guards his books, including this one. He fears that a copy might distort the words and meanings of the Scriptures."

"I understand that, Father."

"Yet we have been told that there is now a copy of the Psalms, coped from the Abbot's book, in our library."

"Yes, Father, there is; but I would say that the Psalms belong to God, not to the Abbot of Kells."

The Abbot held up a hand in warning. "Just answer my statement. There is a copy in our library?"

"Yes there is."

"How did you manage it? It has remained in the dining room throughout its time here."

"It has," Columba nodded.

"No one was permitted to read it except at our meals."

"That is true."

"Then how. . ."

He paused and waited for Columba to respond.

"You know the novice, Brother Cornelius," Columba said.

"Of course."

"You may not know that he has absolute recall. Anything he hears or sees he remembers in its entirety. I learned this during our study sessions. One day I recited a Scripture passage and asked him to interpret it. He repeated it to me word for word, even though it was lengthy, before he began his interpretation. I tested him on this talent several times, and I found that his ability is without limits. He can remember every word, exactly as it is spoken to him, and he can reproduce every word perfectly. He can even repeat passages exactly even after a week's time."

"So you. . ."

"I appointed him to the task of listening to the Psalm that was read each night, reciting the words of it back to me slowly after dinner, and as he recited it I copied it down. That is why we have an exact copy in our library."

"I see."

"There was no danger of perverting the text. It has been reproduced in its pristine purity, just as it came from the pen of David, who heard it from the very mouth of God."

"Well," the Abbot said, glancing at his two associates, "I guess both you and Brother Cornelius deserve to be disciplined."

"No, Father," Columba said, "only I deserve that, if you think the offense is worthy of punishment. Brother Cornelius was only following my instructions. He was learning the rule of obedience to his superiors."

"Columba," the Abbot said with a sigh that rattled in his throat, "can you explain why you did this?"

Columba took a deep breath, collecting his thoughts, and prepared to deliver his defense, a defense he knew would not excuse his behavior but would obey the command to explain.

He was an unusually handsome man. He held himself erect, proudly, despite the attempt to assume the humble appearance of a simple monk. His facial features reflected the aristocratic background of his noble family. He was related by blood to the last several High Kings of Ireland, and had he not chosen the monastic vocation he might one day have been chosen himself to occupy the loftiest throne of Ireland, the one on the Hill of Tara.

As with all young men of royal blood, he was trained in the arts of war. By the age of ten he could ride horseback and handle swords of various sizes and shapes, instruments of war his people had learned from the Romans who occupied the large island to the west. Being larger than most of the boys his age, he entered the battlefield in behalf of his family honor early in life, and by the time he was eighteen he was an experienced soldier. He was only twenty one when a High King died and his family and its dependents went to war with a rival faction of the royal family tree for the throne; but he was given command of a division of foot soldiers.

Unlike other commanders, who simply sent their minions against the enemy without strategy, hoping they could kill more of the enemy than the enemy killed of them, Columba carefully planned his battles, studying the terrain on which they would be fought, assessing the strengths and weaknesses of his enemies, planning how best to attack their weakest points with his greatest strength. He was therefore the most successful of the commanders, and when his clan won the war and his oldest cousin became High King, he was honored as a hero. Men of influence began to think of him as the leading candidate to be the head of his family—and even High King—when his cousin should pass from this earthly sojourn.

Yet in the hour of his greatest victory Columba was miserable. Just as he had carefully planned each battle, so he had instructed his soldiers to keep count of how many men died in each theater of the war. When peace came and he received all of the reports, he calculated that he had been responsible for the deaths of 666 men, two thirds of them the enemy, one third his own soldiers. Despite the fact that he was victorious, he was shocked at the loss of life; and the calculated number itself frightened him. He knew from the instructions he had received in the Scriptures that 666 was the Satanic number.

Columba was a Christian. His family had been Christian for a century. They were among the very first to accept the faith which the beloved Patrick had brought to Ireland from Wales in the fifth century.

Columba's great great grandfather had been in service to the High King on Tara that spring when Patrick lit the Pascal Fire on the Hill of Slane. The only open fire permitted at that time of year was the King's Fire on Tara. Patrick knew this, and lighting his own Fire was a direct challenge to the authority of the King. The King sent Columba's ancestor across the moor to punish the lawbreaker, and on Slane his forebear met the bold young missionary.

As soon as he reached Slane, he asked the small group of men gathered around the fire what they meant by this outrage.

A voice came from the group, "This is a Pascal Fire," it said, "lighted to announce and celebrate the resurrection of Jesus Christ."

He had no idea what the word Pascal meant or who Jesus Christ was, but he let these things pass and went to the heart of his reason for coming from one hill to the other.

"Who is responsible for this transgression of the King's law?" he asked.

A young man stepped out of the crowd and said, "I am."

The man spoke Gaelic with a Roman accent. His was the voice that spoke of the Pascal and the Jesuschrist.

"Who are you?" Columba's ancestor asked.

"My name is Patricio," the man replied calmly.

"What do you mean doing this?"

"I have told you. The fire is to celebrate the resurrection of our Lord and Savior Jesus Christ."

"Resurrection? What do you mean, resurrection?"

"He was crucified, died, and rose from the dead."

"Where is he? Let me see him."

"He has returned to His Father in Heaven. You can see Him only with your heart in your prayers," Patricio replied with a smile.

"Did you not know that it was against the law, lighting this fire?"

"Yes, I knew that. I lived here, in this land, as a slave when I was a boy."

"You were a slave?"

"I was kidnapped and taken from my home in Britain when I was a lad of 12, tending my father's sheep by the sea. I was a slave here until I was 19, when I ran away, hid myself in a cargo of hunting dogs being shipped to Britain, and made my way back to my father's house. While I was away my family accepted the faith of Jesus Christ, and I too became a Christian. At 25 I felt a calling from God, that I was to return to Eire, of my own free will, to bring the true faith to the very people who once so abused me."

Columba's ancestor was impressed by the man and his story, but he had a duty to perform. "You must come with my party," he said.

"To see the King?"

"Yes."

"Good. That was my hope."

So it was that Columba's ancestor walked Patrick and his motley crew of followers the five miles down the Hill of Slane, across the moor, and up to the Hill of Tara to meet the King. He listened as Patrick preached to the King a sermon about the crucifixion, the death, and the resurrection of this person named Jesus Christ, who Patrick said was the Son of God.

That King was not convinced. It was the next High King, his son, who went down into the waters of baptism. But long before that happened, while Patrick and his followers were being held in prison, Columba's ancestor went daily to visit Patrick, listen to his stories, and observe the Christian group share bread and wine. Within a month, before his term of personal service to the High King was over, he had become a Christian. So it was that Columba's family was among the first Irish converts to the new faith. This gave Columba great prestige in the monastic community.

Alongside his military training, Columba was given a Christian education and taught the Scriptures from childhood. He loved the Holy Books, read them over and over, and took their messages to heart. It was in their pages that he learned that the taking of human life was a sin. It was there that he came to understand that the number 666 was the sign of Satan.

So after the war Columba fell into deep despair. He fully believed that his soul was lost. He believed that even though he had fought for the honor and survival of his family, he had committed a sin, a horrible sin, an unpardonable sin. He believed that unless he made atonement he would die and go to hell. That is when he took the long journey, barefoot, in the dead of winter, southward to the Community in the Valley of the Two Lakes and offered himself as candidate for a monastic life. He wanted to leave the world and dedicate the rest of his life to saving souls. He set as his goal the number 666.

"Columba?" the Abbot said.

"What?" Columba roused himself from his memories.

"You were about to explain your behavior."

"Oh. Yes. I. . .have been here for ten years, Father Abbot."

"Yes. I remember when you came. We asked Glen-da-lough for five of their best men to come and help us start our institution. You were one of those five. I welcomed you myself."

"You did, Father. And I hope you believe I have served you faithfully and well. I hope. . ."

"Oh, rest assured that before this incident, I found not a single fault with you. You have been the ideal monk, Columba. That is why I made you Master of Education. I wanted your faith, your zeal, your dedication, your learning to inspire the young men just coming to join us."

"Thank you, Father. But your kind words about my faith, my zeal, my dedication, my learning, these all point to the reason for my actions concerning the Book of Psalms. You see, I believe that the more we Christians know, the more we read and learn, the stronger our faith will be. We have few books here compared to the ones I read at Glen-da-lough. We have only our copy of the Four Gospels, none of the Epistles, no copy of Genesis or Leviticus, no Apocalypse. We need more Holy Books to read.

We need the Psalms, we need the Proverbs, and we need the Prophets."

"Yes. Perhaps so."

"No, Father, definitely so. This is why I broke the rules, why I asked Brother Cornelius to dictate the Psalms to me, why now we have a copy for all the brothers to read. I believe I did something bad in order to do something good."

The room was silent. Columba could hear the breathing of the three men who had already pronounced judgment on him. Father Abbot's breathing was the loudest of the three. His nose whistled when he inhaled, and his throat gurgled when he exhaled. He was a sick man, perhaps a dying man, in an age when colds could take away men in the middle years of life.

"Columba," he said at last. "What we say and do in this room will never be disclosed to the rest of the community. No one here, no one in any other Abbey, no one out in the world will ever know the contents of our deliberations. All they will know is our decision." He turned slightly away from Columba, toward the other two monks, and cast his eyes toward the window, giving his next words an air of objectivity. "I do not condemn you for what you have done. Personally I understand why you did it; and in my heart of hearts I agree with your contention that we need as many books as we can obtain—and that reading them will make our faith stronger."

Columba felt a stirring in the room, and when he glanced at the other two men he saw puzzlement. Father Abbot glanced at them as well and put their views into words for them. "Others disagree. They believe God's Word is precious and might be misinterpreted by inexperienced readers, and they think it should be carefully guarded—held in trust by the wise and learned, interpreted for the simple minded by those who have the wisdom and education to do so."

Columba shook his head and spoke directly to his Abbot. "You know that I disagree with those men, Father. You have heard me speak on the matter. I believe that God's Word speaks plainly and clearly and will always be interpreted correctly if it is read openly and without biased interpretation."

"You do not fear heresy?"

"I fear heresy less than I fear ignorance. In fact, I think heresy is most often the result of ignorance, not of knowledge."

"Yes. I understand you; I find myself coming down on your side; but others do not. In any event, let that argument pass. My major concern at present is that what you have done has soured our relations with the Abbey of Kells. You are an impediment to good relations with them."

Columba waited for the verdict in his case, which he knew was about to come. "We have decided that you must go away."

Columba was stunned. He had expected punishment, some kind of discipline, perhaps he would be stripped of his position as Master of Education, perhaps the library copy of the Psalms would be burned; but he had never anticipated that he would be expelled from the Community. "You mean that I must renounce my vocation, return to the world?"

"No. I cannot demand that of you. Only you can decide to renounce, only you can decide to leave the monastic life. You will remain a monk as long as you so desire, and as long as you are a monk, you will continue to follow our rule. But you must leave this particular place."

"But. . .where will I go? Every Abbey on Eire will know that I have been sent away in shame."

"On Eire, perhaps. . .but there are other islands."

"Other islands?"

"I have been in correspondence with your uncle, your mother's oldest brother, who is still alive and in good health."

"With Killian?"

"Yes. Killian. You were once very close, he tells me."

"He raised me, after my own father died. He became my second father."

"I told him about your difficulties. Rest assured he loves you and wants what is best for you."

"Of course, he would."

"He has made an offer. He is proprietor of an island, a very small island, it is called Iona, just off the coast of the larger island of Mull, which is off the coast of Britain, the northern part named for the Irish tribe that settled there, the Scutti. It is small enough to circle on foot in about two hours. Killian has proposed to give the isle to you, as a place for you to establish a new institution, a place where no one need know of your transgression here. I approve because it is safe from invasion, being an island, yet close enough to send missionaries out to the people in Britain."

"Do the people in Britain need missionaries?" Columba said. "After all, our own Patrick came from there."

"Yes, but across from Iona are the Picts, who have never embraced the True Faith. They go into battle stark naked, with their bodies covered with pictures, painted in garish colors, thus their name. They are barbarians of the least civilized sort, yet their souls are precious to God. They need to hear the Gospel. Then further south the old British people, many of whom are indeed Christians, have been overcome by invaders from the continent, the Saxons, who are also barbarians, not as primitive as the Picts but unregenerate also. No, Columba, there are multitudes to save. I would suggest you set a goal of 666." Father Abbot turned back to Columba and smiled.

"So you know my earlier shame," Columba said.

"I know your earlier vow, to save 666 souls. Have you fulfilled it?"

"No. Everyone who comes to the Abbey is already saved."

"Then your Uncle Killian and I are doing you a great favor. We are giving you the opportunity to reach your goal."

"Yes," Columba said. I can see that. Thank you, Father. Please also get word to Uncle that I am grateful to him as well."

"I will."

The abbot rose, as did the other two members of the tribunal.

"You will leave in two days time. I am sending two of the brothers, Ezekiel and Joshua, to accompany you in your crossing. They both have experience at sea. They will help you get established and then return to us here, leaving you to attract followers of your own, men who know nothing of what has happened in Eire, men who can help you build a new Community."

"Thank you, Father." Columba bowed to the Abbot and to the other two monks. As he opened the door, the Abbot spoke: "God be with you, my Son."

"Thank you, Father," Columba said. "I trust He will be."

III

One of the other monks drove me to New York; and I flew from there to Scotland on Icelandic Airways, which during the flight I dubbed the Greyhound of the Sky. That tells you something about Icelandic and about the Abbey's finances. Father Abbot wanted me gone but did not want to spend much money on my trip. My plane, filled mostly with money strapped college kids, landed briefly in Iceland to let off fifty or so natives, then at the airport near Glasgow, Scotland, where it let me and a dozen others off before taking off again for Luxemburg, the deepest it was permitted to penetrate the Continent. The air smelled a great deal sweeter in the airport than on the plane, filled with students who either couldn't afford or preferred not to use deodorant.

I was dressed in jeans and a well worn sweat shirt, both covered as best I could do it with a longish, all purpose waterproof jacket, without any religious insignia, what I call my "civvies." I left my "clerics" at home, knowing that a man dressed in Roman Catholic monastic or even priestly garb would stand out in the land of John Knox. His Calvinists had run priests out of their churches, broken out stain glass windows, smashed sacred images to sand, and introduced congregational hymn singing and interminable sermons to a people once quite Catholic. Scotland had become the home of Presbyterian Predestinationalism. I doubted that a Catholic priest would be skinned alive these days, as a few had been in the sixteenth century; but I also doubted that

I would be able to find a Catholic church in that part of Britain, and I thought it best not to raise eyebrows.

Not that I didn't stand out wearing my "civvies." A paunchy guy in his late 60s looks strange in a robe, but he looks even stranger dressed like a kid in jeans and sweat shirt. Oh yes and a red baseball cap with a blue B on it. I took a chance on wearing my Boston cap because I figured few people in Scotland would know what the B stood for and/or have strong opinions about the Red Sox, the team I live and die with, mostly die.

I am not a comfortable flyer, and so I was physically deflated by the sleepless overnight trip. I went immediately to a hotel in Glasgow City and conked out for twelve hours. It was nearly midnight, Sunday night turning to Monday morning, when I awoke, made myself understood well enough in an all night greasy spoon restaurant near the hotel to order fish and chips with a pint of the local beer, McEwen's I seem to recall, and then with my stomach complaining went back to bed but slept only fitfully the rest of the night. Still dyspeptic at 7:00, I eschewed the free hotel breakfast, checked out at 8:00, and got to the bus station in time for a 9:15 bus to Oban. After I boarded the bus I remembered that I had missed mass the day before, but I figured one Sunday in a lifetime would not send me to hell. I would have to say my own mass the next two Sundays anyway.

The Scottish brogue of the hotel clerk, the ticket agent, the driver, and my fellow passengers on the bus was so thick that I had to ask almost everyone who spoke to me to repeat himself or herself at least once. It was as hard to understand as the Black English I had encountered in Mississippi or the "Korglish" spoken in Seoul. I would learn later than the people in this region say they do not speak English, they speak Scots. Whether that is a separate language is debatable, but it certainly is a separate dialect. If you don't believe me, read some Robbie Burns some night. The best laid schemes gang aft aglee, right.

Despite the fact that accent, theirs and mine, kept me apart from my fellow travelers, I enjoyed the ride to Oban. I found the countryside that I saw out the bus window to be among the most beautiful in the world. There had been heavy rains, and the hills were spouting waterfalls. The lakes we passed were clear and sparkling, and the grass grew green and lush all the way down to the edges of the waters. Scotland is a fair land.

My only concern was that, with the change in time, I didn't know when to take my blood pressure pill. Was noon in Scotland the same as early morning in Pennsylvania? Just to be safe I took out one of the bitter little things and gathered enough saliva to wash it down, and swallowed it as I bounced along.

I reached Oban just in time to walk across the road from the bus stop, my small valise swinging at my side, and catch an outbound ferry to the Isle of Mull. There I caught a bus that took two hours to go 26 miles, literally on a one lane road, to the tiny seaside hamlet of Fionphort, which lay just across a narrow body of water from Iona. The ferry across to Iona launched each half hour, and I had some time to look across at the place I would call home for the next three weeks. I could see three small hills above a wide expanse of land reaching down to the sea. As I had been told, the island appeared to be less than two miles long north and south, and though I couldn't see the opposite shore, the books said it was less than a mile wide east to west. There were only a few buildings, among them what appeared to be a church, which was the only building made of stone. It was gray while the other few structures, all wood frame, were white.

The twice hourly ferry arrived back from Iona and picked me and a dozen other pilgrims up at 4:00, and I was on Iona fifteen minutes later. Following directional signs, I walked up from the jetty, turned right, passed the ruins of what was described on a sign outside as the ruins of the Benedictine Convent, and headed up to the Abbey, a short walk. I went through a gate and passed a cemetery which was described by another sign as the burial place of kings, and went into the building. A woman who proved to be all smiles and small talk stood up from a desk near the door and welcomed me. I gave her my name, and she nodded curtly, smiled, and led me up a stairway, talking constantly, giving me all the rules and regulations and opportunities attached to what she called The Community. Her brogue was not quite as thick as the ones I had been hearing, but it was distinctly Scottish.

We came to a door, which she opened. "This will be yourrrs," she said. She pointed to a slot on the door, and in the slot was a card with my name on it. I was "Father Columba." The title seemed not to bother her. She stepped aside, and I looked into a small room, sparsely furnished, with a bed, a sink with a single cup on it, a table with a lamp, and a chair.

I guess I looked surprised, perhaps disappointed, because she said, "You're a Catholic monk, aren't you?"

"Yes I am."

"Then you're used to such as this, am I right?"

"Uh, well, more or less."

"You're lucky. The rooms here in the Abbey are nicer than the ones in the Community's Fellowship Hall."

"I see."

"Since you are single—and will be with us for a longer time— we put you here. There are only four rooms here in the abbey. Just you and three others are here. The other 28 guests are across the road. As I say, you're lucky."

"Yes. Well, thank you."

"Someone will bring you a pot of refreshment every afternoon at three. Would you like tea or coffee?"

I thought for a moment. When in Britain. . . "Tea," I said.

"Tea it is. Have a nice stay."

"I'll make an effort."

She started to leave; then she turned back. "Oh, I forgot to brief you. We have a Vespers Service in the chapel at 5:30, if you want to join us, of course that is optional; and dinner is at 6:00, in the refectory downstairs, followed by our discussion group, again if you want to join us."

"Thank you."

"Not at all. You'll hear bells."

"That I *am* used to."

I watched her go and then went into my room and closed the door. I noticed there was no way to lock it. Even at a monastery, where everyone knows everyone, we have locks on our doors. These people were showing either a lot of faith in or a lot of ignorance of human nature. I unpacked my small case, hung up my extra sweat shirt, put my change of underwear in the desk drawer, arranged my toiletries on the small sink, and lay down on the narrow bed. It was not the most comfortable mattress I could have wished to have, but I had no trouble falling immediately dead asleep. I might have slept until midnight again had the promised bells not awakened me just before 5:30. It was time for what they called Vespers. I got up, washed my face, rinsed out my mouth, and found my way down the stairs to the chapel.

The service was brief and self consciously nonsectarian. A reading from the Old Testament, then one from the New, some inspirational poetry, followed by a prayer that would offend no one, not even Satan. I spent most of the half hour looking around at the architecture. The floor was original, made of native stone, but from about half way up the walls the building had been reconstructed at the good graces of the local laird of beloved memory. Books I had consulted said that during the Reformation the King of England had the roof removed, to extract the lead, and that weather and locals looking for building blocks for their houses and hedge rows had taken the walls halfway down. At one time cows and horses ruminated across the sacred altar. The pews were restorations but were roughly hewn to give the look of the Middle Ages. All in all it was a pleasant place. It was just no longer Catholic.

I did give a cursory glance or two at the other "worshippers," about two dozen of them it appeared. If there were 32 rooms and they were all filled, some were skipping the service. The ones there all appeared reasonably young and earnest and well nourished. They kept silence as they filed out of the chapel and down the hallway to the refectory, but once they were seated there they became chatty. There were four tables, all fully engaged, eight persons to each, which meant a few who had cut the service had decided not to cut the meal. The ones at my table introduced themselves to me, but I was still in too deep my jet lag fog for the names to register. They asked me a lot of questions and tried to make me feel welcome. They all seemed anxious to show good will and prove themselves open to greater religious understanding. I began to feel a bit better about spending a few days there. I noticed that a clean cut young man at another table kept glancing at me, and once he smiled and nodded. I returned the nod, not knowing what it meant.

I went with the diners to the discussion session, where there were even fewer bodies than at the Vespers service, but I was so sleepy I couldn't really follow the line of thought. A young man, perhaps in his mid 30s, introduced the theme of the night, something about "The New Morality," but neither he nor anyone else seemed to know much about it, and my mind wandered. After a time I whispered my excuses to a young lady sitting beside me, nodded an apology to the discussion leader, miming somnolence, and left for my room and bed.

I was passing the chapel when I heard a familiar Voice: "SO YOU MADE IT—ALL THE WAY TO IONA."

"Yes," I said. I was feeling a bit lonely, being I suspected the only Catholic in the establishment, so I welcomed a bit of company, even His. At least God is a Catholic. I went into the chapel and sat down.

"WELL, WHAT DO YOU THINK?"

"Of what, this place?"

"YES. IT'S CALLED THE HOLY ISLE? DOES IT GIVE YOU A PIOUS FEELING?"

"Not yet. What I'm feeling now is exhaustion."

"GIVE IT TIME. PEOPLE WHO STAY HERE FOR AN EXTENDED PERIOD SAY THEY FEEL THE PRESENCE OF GOD IN THIS PLACE."

"I feel that every place. You're hard to shake."

"THANK YOU. THAT'S GOOD TO KNOW."

"Tell me, is there any really good reason I'm here?"

"MAYBE."

"Will I be able to use my priestly gifts among these Protestants? The way they look at me makes me think I'm to be tolerated but not trusted, more a curiosity than a member of the Community."

"WE'LL FIND SOMETHING USEFUL FOR YOU TO DO."

I didn't like His tone. "Like what?"

"I'M THINKING."

"Good," I said. While You are thinking, I'm going to bed."

"SEE YA." He said it with a Scots brogue. Cute.

I went upstairs, found the communal washroom, and took a quick shower. Not being able to lock my door worried me, but the minute I say down on my narrow bed I was fast asleep.

* * *

For the second time, just before 6:00 the next morning, I was awakened by bells. I washed my face in my sink, pulled on my clothes, and went down the hall and made use of the community john without encountering anyone there. The lady has said there were three other people on my floor, but so far I had not seen or heard any of them there. They seemed not to touch the floor when they walked and needed not to bath or relieve themselves. Strange. I went into the dining room and was puzzled not to see any of the guests, only the cook.

"Uh, am I too early?" I asked her.

"No, not to help me," she said. This woman's accent was pure Scots, thick and harsh, but I was getting accustomed to it, and I followed her reasonably well. "The otherrrrs are havin' prrrayers," she said. "Guess somebody forrrgot his assignment this morrrnin', wouldn't ya know?" She pointed toward the cupboard. "You can set the tables, that'll be your chorrre for the day."

I shrugged and went over and picked up plates and eating utensils and began setting the tables. The woman smiled. "You act like you've done this beforrre."

"Oh yes," I said. "I live in an abbey. I'm a Catholic priest."

"Oh arrre ya?" She stood back and observed me, the way she might have observed a new kind of animal at the zoo. "Well, isn't that something."

"Yes, it's something."

A man came rushing into the room, apologizing profusely, saying he had forgotten he was supposed to set the tables; and the cook informed him he was too late for that but that he could come stand behind the counter and serve people as they filed past with their breakfast trays. She thanked me for the contribution I had made to breakfast, meager as it was, and told me to take a seat, that I had done enough for the moment. I couldn't tell whether I was being treated special, and if so whether it was because of my age or my religion.

I took a seat at one of the tables, and soon I found myself surrounded by eight others, four men and four women. I could tell from their accents, in the few words they exchanged, that they were Americans. The table was supposed to seat only eight, but my new companions managed to squeeze in. I have observed that in general Americans do not like to touch each other, except to mate, but these Americans seemed not to have any aversion to it. One of the men, the one who had eyed me during dinner the night before, offered me his hand and introduced himself: "I'm Wes Kelly," he said as we shook. "I know that you are the famous Father Columba."

"Columba, yes, that's right," I said. "Have we met?"

"No, oh no. I saw your name on the guest list, and I recognized it. I know something about you."

"You do? What? How?"

"You've been covered in the *Christian Century*, which I read faithfully every week. It carried accounts of your work in Mississippi and in Korea. No picture, but all I needed was to see your name. Those murder cases. They were very interesting. I'm something of a murder mystery buff, in addition to being a pastor. I consider myself a fan of yours."

"Oh well, I stumble along."

"I'm pastor of Calumet Stables Methodist church in Lexington, Kentucky. These people are all from my parish, come for the spiritual renewal here on Iona. People, this is the famous Father Columba." His people looked at me without recognition. Apparently the pastor was the only *Christian Century* reader in his church. Wes Kelly gestured around the table as he introduced his bloc of communicants. "Father, those are the Johnsons, Marilyn and Jack. Those are the Harrisons, Julie and Ralph. Those are the Joneses, Patti and Eric." Each couple smiled and nodded as their names were called but said nothing. There was one woman without a man. I thought perhaps it was Reverend Kelly's wife, but he corrected that assumption. "This is Beth Edwards, but we seem to be missing her husband Tom." He looked at the woman with raised eyebrows. "Beth, maybe you'd better go see about him. Tell him we leave for Staffa in an hour."

Without speaking, Beth Edwards made a last few chews on her mouthful of toast, took a swig of her tea, and with an exasperated sigh got up and left the table. Wes Kelly went on to explain that all the members of his group were music teachers, a couple at the university, a couple at the community college, four in the public schools. "They are also my choir," he said with a happy smile. "Rather than having the usual amateurs drawn from congregational volunteers, we have an octet, and they are terrific," he told me. "You never heard a sour note from our choir loft."

"I see," I said. "That must be nice. We have a few tone deaf monks at Saint Vincent's. That's where I live."

"Oh yes, I know that." He laughed happily. "I've thought of coming there on a retreat, hoping to meet you. But now I don't have to." Then he explained that his group had been on Iona for a week and would be there another six days, a longer stay than the week most groups took. "But this is not only a time to develop a deeper spirituality but a reward for the long hours and hard work my choir has put in for the last three years. They deserve it." He smiled at his group, and I gathered from their tepid response that they thought they did not deserve quite so long a reward. Some of them looked like they were good and ready to go home this morning.

He explained that they had put in a good, strong, healthy week of worship and meditation and that the outing to the nearby island of Staffa would be sort of like a mini vacation. "Staffa is famous in Celtic folklore," he explained to me, as obviously he had to his group because they were not listening. "It was formed by a prehistoric volcanic explosion, and the sea has carved out what appear to be columns all around it. The Vikings gave it the name Staffa, since their word for a column was something like a staff. It has a grotto called Fingal's Cave, also carved out by the sea swells. Celtic legend says it was carved by the Irish giant Finn McCool, who also threw down the so-called Giant's Causeway off the coast of Northern Ireland. I hope the sea isn't too choppy for us to go into the cave—as well as go up on top and see the Puffins. They are said to be quite a spectacle."

He talked constantly as the others ate, turning from telling me about Staffa and the outing they were about to undertake to telling his followers about my murder cases. I was embarrassed by his unending cascade of compliments—they reminded me of the waterfalls I had seen on the way over to Iona. He encouraged the others to ask me questions, and they made an effort, but it was obvious that they were really not interested. Musicians are not in general enthusiasts for murder mysteries. They like things clearly delineated, without surprises waiting on the next page. Beethoven might have been an exception.

I was glad when the general lack of enthusiasm for my exploits led Wes at last to drop the subject and talk about himself. He said he was sorry his wife had been unable to come, she was expecting their second child, and she would so much have enjoyed meeting the famous monastic detective. I was afraid he might take up my stories again, so I quickly finished my modest repast and excused myself. He called to me as I headed for the door, "Hope to talk with you soon." I smiled and waved goodbye to him. His parishioners continued to eat in silence as he turned to them to go on with his monologue.

As I passed the front door I saw Beth Edwards coming back to the Abbey from the white frame Fellowship Hall across the road, where I assumed the Kentuckians, being a fairly large group, were lodged. She was alone. I wondered if she had found her husband. I assumed the rooms over there were singles like the ones in the Abbey and that is why she did not know until she got to breakfast that her husband was not up and about. Apparently he still wasn't; but since she didn't look concerned I also assumed she had found him safe and well. Poor man, perhaps he was still jet lagged, like me, but that seemed strange after he had been across the waters for a week.

I saw few of the Community people the rest of the day. They all seemed to be away on outings, the way the Kentuckians were. The dining room provided no lunch, so participants were on their own from breakfast to dinner. I spent the morning walking around the island along the seashore, and it proved true, as I had been told, that a person could make the journey, if he walked spritely, in two hours. I dawdled, and it took me four. I had mussels at a little seafood shop in the tiny town by the jetty, served up by the proprietor who told me to call him Adam, then reversed my steps and walked back around the island the other way. Around on the west side of the island, guess who?

"GETTING A BIT ITCHY?"

I looked out at the sea. Swim that way far enough and I would reach Canada. "I could go stir crazy here."

"IT'S HOW NAPOLEON FELT ON ELBA."

"I know the story."

"HE WAS WILLING TO RISK DEATH TO GET OFF THAT ISLAND, AND IT'S A LOT BIGGER THAN THIS ONE."

"I know, I know. I teach history. Are You trying to comfort me?"

"I PREFER TO CHALLENGE, NOT COMFORT."

"This is a challenge."

"RELAX, ENJOY THE SOLITUDE, IT MAY NOT LAST."

"What do You know that I don't."

"A LOT. ACTUALLY I KNOW EVERYTHING."

"All right, now that we are in a Calvinist land, predestination and all, tell me the truth. Do You know the future?"

"OF COURSE."

"Then what you know will happen has to happen."

"WELL. . ."

"No, come on. If you know the future, then what you know has to happen, and therefore human life is predetermined, we are predestined. We do not have free will. Calvin was right."

"THAT IS NOT GOOD CATHOLIC THEOLOGY."

"That's not what I asked. Do we have free will?"

"WE'LL TALK ABOUT IT SOMETIME."

"Right."

He would never talk about it sometime. He never comes back to discuss a topic when I have Him cornered.

IV

Roosters were crowing in the Abbey's foreyard as Columba took his leave of what had been his home for a decade, at sunrise on a warm summer's Monday morning. He left early in part because he had a long journey to the coast and in part because he didn't want to say goodbye to his brothers. At this hour they would be in the chapel for prayer, before entering the hall for breakfast. Father Abbot came out of the front gate with the two monks who would accompany Columba overland and then across the waters to his new home. They had both been fishermen in an earlier life and knew the sea. Although they would all three be ferried by experienced sailors, it was wise to go with men who understood the unpredictable ways of the ocean. These two men had orders to go with Columba to the Isle of Iona but then return immediately to the Abbey. The Abbot did not want anyone in Columba's new home to know his past.

"God be with you, Columba," Father Abbot said.

"I pray He will," Columba responded.

Father Abbot did not embrace Columba. The pain of separation was too great for them both. He simply made the sign of the cross on his own breast and expressed it outwardly toward Columba.

The three monks set off, and Columba looked back only once, as they topped the last hill visible from the Abbey. Father Abbot was still watching them, but he did not wave, and Columba turned toward the east and started down the hill, forever out of the sight but not out of the hearts and minds of his brothers left back in Ireland. In the years ahead the Abbey would obtain many more books and Columba's dream of a good library would be realized, but he would never know this, and he would not be given credit for it.

The journey to the coast took two days and nights, and the large sail boat that was waiting for them there took three more days to cross the sea to Iona. Columba's Uncle Killian had arranged for the passage, and it went through without flaw. The sea was as still as a lake, and the sickness Columba feared, having heard tales from men who had crossed to Scotland, never came. It was mid-afternoon of the sixth day of travel that the boat entered the strait between Mull on the right and Iona on the left. Columba went to the prow and caught his first look at his new home, his place of exile, the tiny dot of land where he was to seek his atonement, where without knowing it he would find fame and achieve sainthood.

He saw a treeless expanse of land that sloped gently down to the sea from a higher backdrop, itself topped by three lumps of rock. He immediately named the lumps Father, Son, and Holy Ghost. Eventually he would give each landmark on the tiny island a sacred name. For the first time on the waters, as they entered the strait, the sea turned choppy. It took the sailors some effort to bring the boat to the shore, but within an hour they had made a landing, beside four small sailboats equipped with oars. Columba and his two brother monks stepped off onto the white sands, crossed the beach, and went upland toward five small huts. The sailors remained with their ship.

An old man, followed by four younger men, emerged from one of the huts and came toward them. None of the five smiled or gave a sign of greeting. The three monks stopped and waited warily as they approached, assuming they were friendly but aware of the dangers human nature posed. Their Abbey in Ireland had been invaded and sacked a number of times by strange bands of looters looking for gold and silver. The monks there were in the process of building a stone tower, with the only entrance four times the height of a man, where they could escape with their valuables and pull a rope ladder up behind them when such marauders came. The five men walking toward them had no weapons and looked harmless, like subsistence farmers who tilled the barren stretch of land around their small gathering of houses, but one could never tell.

"Would one of you be Master Killian's son?" the old man asked. Columba realized from the way he stared at them without focus that he was blind.

"I am Killian's *nephew*," Columba said. "My name is Columba. The two men with me are my traveling companions. They will not be staying, only I. They will leave tomorrow."

"Yes. Columba," the old man said. "That is the name in the message the Master sent me. He told me you now own the island. That means you are my new Master and I am your most loyal servant. Adam MacAdam is the name. These are my four sons. We are tenants here, farming the land at your pleasure, Good Master. Tell us what you desire. My sons are strong and able, and their wives are good cooks and washerwomen."

"Did my uncle inform you of my vocation?" Columba asked.

"He said you were a monastic," the old man said. "We have built you a lodging, where to sleep. It is just for the time. We will make it bigger."

"All I need is a roof over my head and a hearth to build a fire for cooking and to keep me warm come winter," Columba said. "I hope to build a Community of monks here, but all in good time. If others come, they will make the house bigger. All you need do is keep the land in good condition, as you have apparently done in the past, and keep strangers from landing here. Just show me where you have put my place, and you can go on about your usual business without further concern for me."

"I need to tell you," the old man said, frowning, "that along with farming, we do a bit of fishing, if that is all right with you, sir."

"That is all right." He had assumed they fished from seeing the boats.

"And I make a pittance, too, by telling fortunes."

"Fortunes?"

"Yea, my sons row me across to the other shore once a week, and those in search of wisdom come and get their fortunes told."

"I guess you know that fortune telling is against Christian teaching, that it is forbidden in the Bible."

"No, that I didn't know. But I tell you, sir, that I give God all the glory for the special insight He gives to me."

Columba was not happy about the old man's answer, but he decided to delay making a decision about whether to stop his soothsaying until he was more fully settled and had looked into the matter. He nodded vaguely and let the topic drop for the time being.

The old man seemed satisfied not to have a further comment on his avocation. He and his sons led Columba and his companions to the north side of the island, where beneath the third rocky mound, which Columba had named Holy Ghost, lay a small hut. It had a front door facing east, windows at each end, a bed, a table and chair, and a fireplace. On the table sat utensils for eating. Columba thanked the old man and his sons and sent them away. He and his companions then settled in to say mass and pray, cook and eat his last communal meal, and spend the evening in the last conversation he would have with monastic brothers for the foreseeable future. He told them that he felt both melancholic and excited. He was sad to leave his past behind but anxious to see what the future held.

The next morning he walked his companions back to the ship and watched as they splashed into the water, went aboard, saluted him, and sailed away to the south. They rounded the end of Iona and were gone, leaving him to God and his fate, to his quest for atonement.

That night, having eaten alone, he said his prayers. "Lord God, I can only trust that You have a purpose in sending me into exile here, to this lonely, lonely island. I will await Your revelation, wait for You to guide me, wait for Your answer to my questions. My soul is as blind as that old man's eyes. I stumble forward, searching for my destiny, for a torch to light my way."

* * *

Ten years passed. For the first of those years Columba lived in solitude. He planted and harvested a garden and prepared his own meals. He prayed alone. He saw the tenants only when he passed their settlement on his walks around the island. At the end of ten years he had eight followers, all vowing to following the monastic rule, a dormitory to house them, a small chapel in which his Community worshiped, a barn for the four cows that provided milk and the two dozen hens that provided eggs, and a large workshop for making products needed for farming, all surrounded by fertile gardens of vegetables and flowers. The growth had been gradual but steady.

The second year he had begun to have visitors, men mostly from Mull just across the strait, then from farther away on the mainland, seeking his counsel. They came singly and in groups of three or four. They told him they had heard of a holy man, a hermit who spent his entire life in prayer, who could reveal to them the will of God for their lives. Columba took pains to explain to them that he had no special revelation, that he himself was struggling to know what God wanted of him and his followers; but his protestations of ignorance were taken to be signs of great humility; and those who came to talk and pray with him took the word back to their communities that indeed a man of holy temperament and divine spirit lived on Iona.

The visitors told him of stories about the various miracles, circulating around the islands, that he was said to have performed.

"Miracles?" he mused.

Yes, they answered, people said that when he first came to Iona the island was inhabited by pagans and that he had challenged them to a duel by fire, to see whose God was strongest, and that Columba's God sent fire from heaven to consume an animal sacrifice, a slaughtered sheep, while their gods did not, and that they were all converted to Christianity.

"That was Elijah," he told them, but his demur did not put an end to the story of his power to bring fire down from heaven.

They told him they had heard Satan came and tempted him with a promise that if he bowed down to the Prince of Darkness he could rule the earth, and that he had resisted the temptation and had sent Satan scurrying off to other islands to tempt other men.

"That was Jesus," he told them, but his denial only increased talk about his humility and power over the powers of evil.

They told him they had heard that once he reached into a pile of firewood and was bitten by a poisonous snake but that he shook the snake off into the fire and was unhurt by the bite.

"That was Paul," he told them.

They told him they had heard that after the bite he had banished all snakes from Iona.

"That was Patrick," he told them.

His protestations and corrections did no good. The stories grew and multiplied and spread his fame across the lands from which his visitors came to meet with him.

He asked the earliest of his visitors how they had heard about these "miracles," and they told him that the blind man's sons had spread the word. He noticed that the sons were spending more and more of their time rowing pilgrims across the strait and back again and less time with their gardening and fishing. At first it was just one day each week that they took their father across and left him to hold court for those who sought his prophesies while they ferried a group over to see Columba, then brought him home when they took the pilgrims back to Mull. Now that Columba had regular visitors they made the trip across to Mull every day. Columba was rapidly becoming their cash crop.

One night as Columba walked past their settlement he heard them discussing their good fortune: God had indeed blessed them by sending them this Holy Man, and they intended to cash in on the revenues. Rowing was much easier than plowing, and they could do it most of the year. As the Holy Man's reputation grew, the fee for crossing increased. Their propaganda was paying great dividends. They laughed when they recounted how one man being ferried back said he felt the stiffness in his arm and leg healed by touching the Holy Man as he left him. They encouraged the man to tell his friends back home. A few more stories of miracles like that would be a boon to their trade.

Columba was disturbed by what he heard, and the next day he told the boys that he would not entertain visitors for a month.

They were obviously disappointed, and three days later they approached his hut to say that the crowd of people waiting on the opposite shore was growing at such a rate that local authorities did not know how to deal with them. Some were threatening to hire other sailors to bring them across if the boys did not do so. Thus Columba relented and permitted the visitors to come, but he limited the numbers, which only made the desire to see him grow stronger.

In the third year a young man had come to see him, talked with him well into the night, and at the end of their conversation, after they had prayed together, asked Columba if he could stay on the island, if he could live with him.

Columba looked into the earnest black eyes. "Why?" he asked the fellow, who was around 25 years old, with talents that could make him a wealthy and prominent man out in the world.

Without hesitation, the young man answered, "I believe you are a man of God. I believe God has called me to follow you, to live here with you. I want to be your disciple and learn from you."

He asked the boy the same questions he had been asked when he volunteered to be a monk.

"You want to take up the monastic life? You want to take the vows?"

"I do."

"You want to promise God—no simple, no flippant promise—that you will remain chaste, that you will live in poverty, that you will obey me no matter what I may ask you to do?"

"I do, Father Columba."

Columba sighed. He had hoped to form a community, yet now that he faced his first convert he hesitated. He would no longer be a hermit, others would come, and he would have to be Abbot. He would have to take responsibility for other men's lives. It would be a burden. Only if he were sure God had called this man to come and live on Iona would he agree to his request.

"What is your profession now?"

"I fish," the boy said. "My family has five boats."

"You stand to inherit them?"

"I do."

"You would give them up, give up your family, give up the prospects of having a wife and children, give up the sea to be a celibate prisoner on this small island?"

"I would, Father, gladly."

"Very well," Columba sighed. "You may stay for the time being. You will not take any vows now. After a month, after a year, who knows how long, perhaps you can then take solemn vows and stay permanently. Until then I could tell you to go and you would have to go, no questions asked."

"Thank you, Father, for the chance to prove my vocation. I know this is what God wants me to do."

Columba let the boy stay, and only two months passed before he was reasonably sure the young man had a true vocation. In less than a year he let him take his vows, and he gave him the name Peter, after the first disciple of Jesus, the man called from fishing in the Sea of Galilee.

Within a few months the word had spread—he was sure the blind man's sons were responsible—that Columba had accepted a disciple; and then there were others, many others, who asked to stay with him. Most he tested and found wanting and told to go back to the world. They were attracted by his celebrity but had no vocation. A few, a very few he accepted, and by the end of his ten years on Iona his small community had the eight members. Having named the first one Peter, he continued by naming each new addition after the next disciple Jesus accepted. The second was Andrew, then James, John, Philip, Bartholomew, Thomas, and Matthew.

As he named them he wondered what he would do if and when he reached number 12. He could not burden a man with the name Judas. He would have to name him Matthias, after the one chosen by the other disciples by lot to replace the disgraced traitor. Then he would perhaps go to Stephen, the first Christian martyr, and then Paul. But that was far in the future. He really did not expect or want that many members. Eight was plenty to build the new structures they needed for worship and living, to tend the garden, tend to the animals, assist him in conducting the mass, handle the pilgrims, and say prayers for all those who requested them from the Community.

Columba had known that being Abbot would bring worries. He had not known how many and varied these worries would be.

The thing that concerned Abbot Columba most about the growth of his fame and the expansion of his monastic family was the apparently inevitable increase in monastic wealth. This seemed to happen everywhere. Monasteries became repositories of gold and silver and thus targets for thieves. First one, then another, then another pilgrim came with gifts to leave behind after meeting and praying with the saintly monk Columba, and the wealth began to mount.

The first gift was a silver cup. It came from an elderly woman, well dressed and obviously prosperous. Columba had established the rule that no woman under 60 years of age could visit the island. Young women were too much of a temptation to his disciples. Very few women were permitted to come on the boat to Iona—and then only if they were old enough not to pose a threat to the men's composure and if every part of their bodies except hands and faces were completely covered with dark clothing.

He had also warned the blind man's sons that their wives must no longer venture outside their huts without being completely covered. In the days when he lived as a hermit he often saw them scantily clad walking about in their yards. On more than one occasion, in warm weather, he saw them walking together from their settlement down to the beach naked. The sight of their large breasts and rumps swaying as they moved across the white sand toward the water's edge pricked his sensations; and he had to pray hard to avoid the temptation of self stimulation as he watched them going in and out of the sea, the salt water streaming down their bodies, over their prominent nipples, through the luxuriant pubic hair between their legs, making their bodies shine like silver shells. They even played games on the beach in which they chased each other and mimicked sex acts to raucous laughter. Once his Community was born, when he had more than one disciple, he forbade them to take such swims except after dark, when the monks were asleep; and he specified that outside their huts they must dress head to toe in black. The women complained about these rules, but their husbands, anxious to please the Master of the Isle and to protect their lucrative business, made them obey.

The elderly lady who brought Columba the first gift told him of her concerns about her son, who she said was dissolute and would be incapable of assuming the responsibilities his wealthy landowning father would leave to him.

"How old is your son?" he asked her.

"He is past 30, but he is still a boy at heart, unable or unwilling to grow up and act like a man. He has not married, and he drinks to excess every night and gambles away our wealth."

"Is you husband in good health?"

"No, he is not, and that is my concern. Should he die, all we have worked for will wither and die. Can you, can God, help me?"

Columba listened attentively to her story, nodding to show that he heard and understood, and then he told her that while he could not provide a definitive solution to her problem, he would pray for her and for her son. He told her that while she should not expect a miracle, and certainly should not demand one, she should put her trust in the Providence of God. She thanked him profusely and assured him that she knew God would hear his prayers, even if He did not hear hers. He extended his hand to bless her, and she grasped it and kissed it. Then she drew the cup from her sleeve and offered it to him. "This is a small offering for you, Father, to show my gratitude," she said.

"Oh no," Columba said, hiding his hands behind him. "I do not require payment. I do not accept gifts. I am but a servant of God, doing what I can to help mankind."

"Of course, Father, I know you do not want pay, and that is why everyone loves you so much. This cup is not to make you rich. I know you will not sell it. I just want you to use it to serve the wine to the brothers in mass. I want to know that it has become a holy vessel for the service of God. God's blood deserves to be distributed in the finest of silver."

Columba hesitated, watching her eyes. Then he nodded. "In that case, and with that spirit, I will accept it. You can be sure that it will adorn the altar during every mass." He took it from her.

"Thank you, Father. Bless your soul."

"Bless yours as well, my Sister."

This was the first of the gifts that began to appear. The elderly woman told others that Columba had accepted her silver cup, and everyone who came, especially the older, wealthier women, sought to surpass her gift with ever richer and more ornate pieces of jewelry or cups and plates. Columba refused them all, but he would find them left behind in the Abbey. The Abbey grew richer; and although Columba tried to keep the gifts a secret and hid them away, people told their friends what they had left, and the word spread about Iona's vast treasure. Columba grew every day more afraid that his Abbey would be attacked and plundered the way the Irish Abbeys had been. It would be easy for thieves to row across the strait, in the middle of the night, and steal the gold and silver he tried to conceal. Or not finding it, they might harm the brothers.

He knew this was the dilemma all communities that tried to turn their backs on the world and its values and live in true Christ like poverty faced. Admirers wanted to honor them for their devotion to the ideals of Jesus, and the only way they knew to do so was give them worldly gifts. Soon they grew rich and spent all of their time protecting the very wealth they had sworn to abandon. They grew corrupt, lost their vocation, and then lost their soul. He thought about selling all the gifts and distributing the proceeds to the poor; but in order to do that he would have to leave Iona and seek out the poor; and then he would have in another way lost his true vocation.

A second concern for Columba was that visitors began bringing with them drawings that were supposed to depict him: his stylized face in the Byzantine pose, representations of him hearing confession, pictures of him laying hands on the sick, something he never did. He was becoming an Icon. He knew that this was the first step toward veneration and that further steps would lead to sainthood; and he knew that with such acclaim always came the danger of pride and the fall from grace that inevitably follows it. He warned his visitors to put these pictures away, not to hang them in their houses, not to pray to them, and to pass this word to their friends. To no avail. The pictures proliferated, and soon they had spread to the whole of eastern Scotland.

A third concern that bore heavily on his mind, beyond Iona's increase of wealth and his own celebrity, was that he would not treat all of his followers equally. He sought to give the eight men who had taken solemn vows as much instruction and guidance as possible—in equal measure; but some were needier, more demanding than others, and he found himself giving some more of his time and attention than others. Some were also more loving then others, and he found it easier to talk with these men, on matters both serious and frivolous, than with others.

He was particularly concerned over his feelings toward John. John was the youngest of the eight, only 17 when he took his vows, and he was the brightest and most promising scholar among them. He was also the most handsome of the brothers, with features almost like those of a fair young girl. He was quick to smile, and his smile lit up a room. When he laughed it sounded like the tinkling of a set of bells. Columba looked forward to seeing him take his place on the front row of pews in the mass and his seat beside Columba at the common table. He truly loved John.

John seemed completely unaware of his virtues. He was without conceit or pride. He was first to volunteer for any task, no matter how onerous it was, no matter how dirty it might make him; and he never gave up on a task, no matter how difficult, until he had finished it. He was the ideal disciple, the ideal monk, the jewel in the monastic crown Columba hoped to fashion.

Columba often took a walk down to the beach between last prayers and his bed time. More than once he met John returning from the seaside as he went down. They would stop and talk; and their conversations always left Columba full of optimism about the future. If he could impart John's spirit to the other men, he would be a successful Abbot, his work would find favor with God.

Yet a doubt crept into his heart. One of the cardinal rules of monastic life was that no one was to have a "particular" friend. This might lead to jealousy and division of the Community. Another rule was that an Abbot must not show favoritism or preference for any one monk over others. Another rule, the strictest of all, was that a monk must never have, exhibit, or express physical longings for another monk.

Columba knew he had never had physical desires for another man, cleric or layman. He remembered how the naked bodies of the MacAdam women affected him, that deep down inside he wanted to have carnal knowledge of one or another or all of them together. Once after watching them bathe and frolic, he had suffered a dream in which they took him with them into the water and joined forces in rubbing their hands over him and encouraging him to rub his hands over them. He was sure he was heterosexual. Thus his confusion about John. He had to admit to himself, and he expressed this admission to God in his prayers, that he truly loved the young man. He hoped this love was born of his natural desire, a desire that could not be fulfilled, to have a son. Yet he had never made love to a woman. He had become a soldier and fought in wars as a teenager; and directly after the Great War he had become a monk. He was a virgin.

John raised terribly confusing issues for him. He prayed that they would be resolved. He prayed that he would always do God's will.

V

I walked a bit faster the rest of the way and got back to the abbey around 2:30, lay down, and took myself a good long nap. I was still jet lagged. Again the bells wakened me, and I went down for the pallid religious service. The crowd seemed small, and as I looked around I noticed that the Kentucky group was missing. I supposed the trip to Staffa must have taken longer than they expected. I was to discover that I was right—but not in the way I thought.

When we all went into the dining room, I took a chair at the table where I had eaten breakfast; but the Kentuckians were still missing, and I found myself sitting alone. After a few minutes the lady in charge of the meal came over to me.

"Father Columba, it appears your friends aren't coming, so why don't you come over and sit at another table?"

"Is there a spare chair at one?" I asked her.

"Yes, over there," she said, pointing to a table. "One of the men from the Edinburgh group is feeling ill, and he will not be coming."

So I moved over and took a chair with a mixed group, half of them from Scotland, half from England. I talked with all of them, and all of them talked with me, but after a few insulting exchanges, the Scottish group would not talk with the English group and vice versa. I suppose as an American I was considered outside the age old feud between the Gaels and the Saxons.

After dinner, since there were still a couple of hours of daylight left, I went out and looked at the stones in the cemetery. Most of the dates were from the late 1700s to the mid 1800s. I had read that most of the stones marking the graves of ancient Scottish and Norwegian kings had been stolen—the few that survived were housed in the Abbey museum—so that no one could say where their bodies lay. Tradition had it that Macbeth was there someplace; but if so his molecules were not marked. He lived now only in Shakespeare; and according to Scottish critics Shakespeare had grossly misrepresented both Macbeth and his history. They said "the Scottish Play" demonstrated what happens when a cockeyed English glove maker writes about a noble Scot.

I was still droopy, and so I was in bed and asleep early, before 10:00 p.m., and what seemed like five minutes later someone knocked at my door. I roused but did not come fully awake. The knock came a second time, louder, more insistent, with more raps. I looked at my little travel clock and was shocked at the time. It was 3:00 a.m. I had been asleep for five hours. I pushed back my comforter and got up. I was stiff from my walk, and I stumbled a bit getting to the door. I opened it a crack and saw the young Methodist pastor Wes Kelly standing next to a largish man in a brown uniform.

"Reverend Kelly?" I said with a yawn.

"Yes, Father Columba. I'm so sorry to disturb you; but I need, we need to talk with you urgently. This is Constable MacDonald."

The big man in uniform bowed slightly and touched the tip of his cap. "Rrron MacDonald," he said.

Oh no, I thought, a constable, what now? I nodded and opened the door wider, but Wes shook his head.

"No, we won't come in. Your room is too small for us all three. Can you come with us down to the dining room?"

"All right," I said. "But why? It's late—or early."

"I know, and I'm sorry, but we have a. . .situation," Wes said.

"That's one worrrd for it," Ron MacDonald said.

I nodded. I didn't ask for more information because I dreaded to know what the "situation" was that needed my attention.

The pastor and the constable stood in the hallway while I pulled on my jeans and sweat shirt and shoes without socks. I wasn't completely sure where my socks were. I came out into the hall, closed my door, noting again that I could not lock it, and followed them down the stairs. On the way down the Constable talked back to me over his shoulder.

"I don't think you can do any good, Padrrre. I'm goin' 'long with this because Mr. Kelly wants you to be brrrought in. Also too because I don't have a clue wherrre to starrrt."

"If I can help. . ."

"Doubt it, but we'll see."

"You'd be surprised," Wes Kelly said. "He's got a good track record."

Then I knew. Someone was dead.

"Like a rrrace horrrse, is he?" MacDonald said with just the hint of a sneer.

I also knew then that I would have to deal with a skeptical local law man, and that was always a tricky business.

We went into the dining room where I found the Kentuckians sitting at the same table where they had eaten breakfast. They looked shocked, frightened, and dead tired.

Uh oh, I thought, this will be no fun.

Wes Kelly and Ron MacDonald remained standing, and so did I. It was obvious something terrible had happened, but I was not going to be the one to ask what it was. I waited as the silence grew more ominous. At last Wes spoke.

"We have lost one of our flock," he said in a funereal tone.

"Murrrderrred," MacDonald said frankly.

"Perhaps," Wes said, glancing at his flock to see their reaction. There was little change in their expressions. "Beth. . .Edwards. . .died this afternoon, on our outing. . .to Staffa."

I looked at the people sitting at the table. There were four men and only three women, the reverse of the group at breakfast. They all looked distraught, but the man I took to be Tom Edward was by far the most bereaved. I had not met him that morning at breakfast, but I assumed he was Edwards by his appearance. I also vaguely remembered the faces of the ones I had met, and his was not one of them. The others looked stunned, but he look devastated.

"What happened?" I asked.

"Well, that is a bit of a mystery," Wes said. "We found her dead on the rocks below the footpath in Fingal's Cave."

"She had fallen?" I said.

"She was prrrobably puuushed," MacDonald said curtly. He had the thick brogue of the Hebrides, but he spoke with some precision, and so I could easily make out what he meant. I guessed he had been away from the area for a time, either at school or in the army, and knew he had to speak distinctly to visitors.

"We don't know that," Wes hurriedly added. "Fortunately she did not fall into the water, or we might still be looking for her. The current was bad today, and she would have been washed out to sea."

"Somebody hit herrr with a rrrock and caused herrr to fall," MacDonald said with certainty.

"We just don't know that," Wes said, turning to face the constable, obviously anxious to establish the fact that he couldn't believe anyone in his flock was a killer.

He turned back to me, his eyes pleading. "Father, we. . .I know of your record, of your ability to cut through irrelevant details and see the truth in such cases, so please help us if you can."

"It's a homicide," MacDonald said. "But I've questioned the whole grrroup, and no one admits seein' a thing. The official line from them is that she wanderrred off alone, while the otherrrs explored different parrrts of the island, and when they went down to the Cave, they saw herrr on the rrrocks below. The sailorrrs who took 'em to the island rrrecoverrred the body and brrrought it back here."

"Where is she now?" I asked.

"Still here," Wes said. "She's lying in state in the chapel. But Constable MacDonald must take her over to Mull on the first ferry of the morning."

I looked at the exhausted group. "Anyone have anything further to say, more than what Mister Kelly and the constable have told me?" I asked.

Six heads shook wearily. Tom Edwards appeared so deep in a trance that he did not respond.

"I think you should all go to bed, and try to get some sleep, although it may be hard," I said. "Nothing more we can do tonight."

Wes vigorously agreed with me and encouraged them to get up and leave the Abbey for their rooms in the Community Center across the road. They obeyed. They made sure Tom Edwards came along with them. Wes stayed behind with me and the Constable. When they had gone, I said, "May I see the body?" MacDonald nodded and led us out of the dining room, down the hallway, and toward the chapel.

"I hope you don't mind if I look into the matter," I said to the constable as we walked, afraid he might be jealous of his territory.

"I don't mind," he said. "But 'th' matterrr' as you call it is strrraight forrrward. "She was hit on the head; and whetherrr the blow killed herrr orrr the fall afterrrwarrrd, whoever hit herrr is rrresponsible."

"I hope you're wrong," Wes Kelly said. "I would like to take my group home as soon as possible—and take Beth's body with us."

"Oh, I don't think it will be soon," MacDonald said. "Not unless one of yourrr parrrishionerrrs confesses—orrr the good Fatherrr is as good as you say."

We entered the chapel and went to the altar, where they had placed Beth Edwards' body on the table. It was covered with the altar cloth, and MacDonald pulled it back to show me her head. Her blond hair was matted and stiff from having been wet with sea spray, and on her forehead was a deep gash, blood encrusted on either side of it but less of it than I would have expected from the depth of the gash.

"Did someone clean the wound?" I asked

"The women tried," Wes said, "on the way back."

"Is this the only wound?" I asked MacDonald.

"Oh hell no," he said. Then he blushed. "Excuse me, Fatherrr, Rrreverend, sorrry about my language."

Both Wes and I demurred.

"No, therrre are brrruises all overrr her body. Do you. . .uh. . .want to look at 'em?"

Again Wes and I demurred again.

"They come frrrom the fall down off the upperrr ledge, the one wherrre people walk to go inside the Cave, down to the ledge where they saw her lyin', where the sailorrrs had to go to bring herrr out."

"Then, could this one have been from the fall as well?" I asked, pointing to the gash on her head.

"Not likely," MacDonald said. "No, not likely atall. In fact I'd say not possible. I know that place in the Cave. The rrrock there is all smooth, no very sharp edges. Plus too, herrr otherrr brrruises are all on her back, like she fell backwarrrd down, and this one is on the frrront of her head. I'd say she was hit and fell. So whetherrr the blow killed herrr orrr the fall, like I said, we have a homicide on ourrr hands."

If MacDonald were right about the Cave, he was right that we had a murder. I groaned inwardly. I didn't need to deal with another one. I had already done two. This would be my third.

The constable covered Beth's head, and we walked up the aisle to the back door. "It's yourrr baby," MacDonald said to me. "Rrreverend here says you have a knack forrr this kind a thing. I don't. I'm a peace officer. I just enforrrce the law. So I'll leave it to you for the time being. Can't wait too long, though, I hate to hold all these people. I need somebody to charge."

"I understand," I said.

We walked out into the church yard. In the distance, down near the beach, we spotted a light. "God damn it," MacDonald said, and this time he didn't apologize. He was obviously incensed. "Come with me," he said, heading toward the light.

When we got to it, we found a young couple lying beside a campfire, deeply involved in the sacred act of love.

"Hey, ye goddammmed fikkin ijjits!" MacDonald yelled. The two came apart, writhing in agony and embarrassment, pulling clothes up and down. "Git the fick outa herrre, doin' that kind a shitey stuff on holy grrround. Go on, git yerrr silly asses outa herrre, ye fikkin ijjits."

The two young people nervously got up and scrambled to get their meager belongings together. MacDonald was gesturing toward the jetty, and they began stumbling in that direction.

"Git on down therrre. Catch the firrrst ferrrry out. Ye can't camp herrre. Don't ya see the signs? Ye should know betterrr, ye fikkin ijjits."

They disappeared into the darkness. MacDonald turned to us and grinned. "Y'll have to excuse the language, men, but I've learrrned that's the only thing they underrrstand. It's more Christian to currrse at 'em a bit than t'make 'em pay a fine. They're all poorr as churrch mice. Betterrr t'scare 'em than t'brrreak 'em. We have signs clearrrly posted about not spendin' the night outside here." Again he grinned. He thought he had a heart of gold.

"Constable, I'll need to go to the place where it happened," I said. "Can you arrange to take me there tomorrow?"

"You want to go to Staffa?" MacDonald stared at me askance.

"I don't want to, but I need to, in order to see the scene of the crime—if there was a crime."

"Are you sure?" Wes put in.

"Yes."

"I need to go too," MacDonald said. "Been a long time since I was on Staffa. I need t'see the spot like you do. I'll rrrequisition a police boat. "Is noon all right?"

"Fine," I said.

"I need t'warn ya, though, the weatherrr forrrecast's not good, not like it was t'day."

"I understand," I said.

MacDonald looked over toward the small village by the dock. A light shone from a window in the café.

"Wonderrr if old Adam has the coffee goin'," he mused. He started off. "If not, I'll make him starrrt a pot. Firrrst tourrrists'll be herrre in a couple hourrrs. They neverrr get enough a Saint

Columba." He walked away, leaving Wes and me at the Abbey gate.

I looked at Wes and shrugged. "There's not much to go on, is there?"

"No," he agreed.

"Do you still say it was an accident?"

"Well, that's what I hope; but what the constable says makes sense; there's the head wound. I just hat to think that one of my people would do such a terrible thing."

"You talked with all of them?"

"Yes, on the island as the sailors were retrieving the body, also on the boat returning, then again in the dining room with MacDonald before we came to get you. They all say they were other places when it happened. Each one was alone, each on a different part of the island, or so they say. I pray to God it was an accident. This will tear our church apart regardless, but a homicide would be catastrophic."

"Maybe," I said. "But I have learned that the Catholic Church can withstand some very heavy assaults, even by its own members. I assume you can say the same thing about the Methodists."

"Yes," he reluctantly agreed. "I think so. Anyway, we must trust in the Lord and His Providence."

"That's the spirit," I said.

He looked exhausted, and I suggested he go to bed. I didn't have my watch, but there was a glow of sunrise over Mull, and I knew it had to be after 4:00.

"Do you plan to call home?" I said.

"Oh gosh, yes," he said, "I hadn't thought about that. "I'll call my wife. I'll get the night guard to let me use the phone in the office. What time is it?" He looked at his wristwatch and did some calculating. She'll still be up. She'll have to tell the church. I'll tell her it was an accident. If we find out differently, I'll then have to change the story, say I was wrong."

"Are there children?"

"Beth and Tom? No. That's probably a blessing. About other family, I really don't know. My wife will see to all that." He sighed. "She'll have to. I can't leave here until everyone else—all the innocent ones—go."

"Why don't we meet at noon, in the dining room," I said.

He looked surprised. "Do you want me to go back to Staffa with you?"

"It would help me if you did."

"In the back of my mind I was dreading that you would ask me to."

"I don't want to insist."

"No, if I must, I will. It was a beautiful place before we found Beth, but then it turned gruesome. Everything seemed to change. Before we found her it was sunny and dry, but then it began to rain, the sea turned choppy, and the rocks were all wet. It became a place of death. That cave became a hell hole." He heaved a big sigh. "Okay. See you at noon then."

He waved farewell and went off toward the office. I doubted he would get much sleep. After he talked with his wife, he would have to make sure that his flock were all in their rooms, tucked in, and then it wouldn't be long before he would be up again.

I felt restless, so I took a long walk, up to the end of the island that faced Staffa. That afternoon I had been able to make out its outline, but now a heavy fog had set in, and I couldn't see it. After a time I ended up back at the Abbey, sitting on the low stone wall that surrounded the cemetery.

"Well, you've done it to me again," I said.

"DONE WHAT?"

"You know. You've involved me in another killing."

"I PUT YOU IN THE PLACE WHERE YOU ARE NEEDED."

"As I said. . ."

"THERE'S METHOD TO MY MADNESS."

"Oh yes? What is it?"

"YOU'RE GOOD AT SOLVING MYSTERIES. I BRING YOU TO THE RIGHT PLACE AT THE RIGHT TIME—SO YOU CAN DO THE MOST GOOD."

"You could of course stop the killings."

"AND THWART MAN'S FREE WILL?"

"Please. Not that again."

"MEN CHOOSE TO DO EVIL, AND I CHOOSE TO BRING THEM TO JUSTICE AND SEE THAT THEY PAY FOR THEIR DEEDS. YOU ARE A PERFECT INSTRUMENT OF MY METHOD."

"Even with all my bumbling?"

"IT'S YOU. IT'S THE WAY YOU WERE MADE."

"The way You made me."

"IF THAT'S WHAT YOU WANT TO BELIEVE. ANYWAY, YOU GET THE JOB DONE."

"Even if it kills me.

The sun was rising, as it did so early in summer among the western islands, sending a silver pathway across the strait from Mull; and as I bumbled my way up the stairs and to my room I could smell breakfast cooking in the kitchen and heard the bell calling people down to the early prayer service and to eat. I decided I could do without prayers and breakfast. Interdenominational prayer had little appeal to me, and Scottish lard sits heavily on a man's stomach. I could sleep better without bland petitions to the Nondenominational Almighty and fried bread, fried eggs, and blood sausages.

I collapsed onto my bed and immediately forgot about the killing and fell into a deep sleep. Unlike the Methodists, I had not seen the body at the bottom of the Cave. Tomorrow night, after I saw the death scene, I would toss and turn the way they were probably doing while I slept. Now I had one last moment of peace.

VI

Columba paid occasional calls on his tenants: the blind man, his four sons, their wives, and the gaggle of children who belonged to various ones of them. He liked to make sure they were following his orders about visitors; and although he knew hardly anything about growing corn or fishing, he felt that as their landlord he should inquire about their husbandry of the land and the waters around it. What they told him the visitors said, about Iona, about Columba himself, often needed correcting, and he was careful to do so, but he never made suggestions about their other methods of livelihood.

It was on one of his visits to the four huts that he first heard the boys talk about the strange island to the northeast of Iona, the one they called "The Forest Isle." They said they went that far out fishing when the sea was at peace, and they talked about its mysterious character. Columba asked if it were the island shaped like a sailing vessel, the one he had seen to the northeast on clear days; and they said yes, that was the one, but that up close it looked like a forest carved in stone. The sides were steep and grooved like tree trunks; and atop these was a profusion of stones shapes like the leaves of tall trees. At one place it looked like a clump of the trees had fallen toward the water. It had caves along the shore—they looked like doors to the center of the earth—which people said had been carved by giants. They told him about a causeway stretching out from the northern coast of Eire. They said that the giants had begun to build a bridge from one island to the other so that they could visit their caves. They had stopped building the causeway and left it falling into the sea because by their efforts they had offended the gods and been forced to abandon their efforts.

Columba listened with great interest. The story the boys told reminded him of the stories he had heard as a youth in Ireland, and those stories reminded him of the one in Genesis, where men had begun to build a great tower that would reach to heaven, only to wake up one morning speaking a confusing variety of tongues and realize that God was offended by their pride and arrogance. They too abandoned their project and scattered to the corners of the earth, each group speaking a language unintelligible to the others. Surely the two stories had a common origin, perhaps a wandering minstrel who told his tale all over the known world, from Palestine to the Celtic islands. Columba was intrigued.

On a subsequent visit to the old man and his sons, he asked if they would take him and his followers to The Forest Isle. The sons gladly agreed and promised him that on a day when the sea was still they would be happy to do so. But their enthusiasm dissipated when they heard their father clear his throat. Columba and the sons looked toward him, sitting by the open fire in the yard before the house where he lived with his five dogs. The sons waited in silence until he spoke.

"This is not good," he said in his simple speech. "It is a mistake to go there, for you, Master, for your followers."

"Why?" Columba asked him. He moved over to stand by the old man's chair. He was now even more intrigued.

"I can't say," the old man said. "The vision is not clear to me. All I know, all I can see in the darkness, is that it not be good. You be sorry."

The oldest of the sons looked at Columba with raised eyebrows and then grinned and jerked his head to the side. His expression indicated that he wanted to have a word in private with the landlord. Columba nodded but held up a finger to tell the boy to wait until he was ready to go.

The son walked Columba back to the Abbey. "He is like that," the boy said. "He warns all his visitors about horrible things that might happen to them; and they go off frightened. I don't know why they keep coming for his revelations, when his predictions are always so dire."

"Some people like to be frightened," Columba said.

"Yes, that be true. But you need not worry. His predictions are right only half the time, and half the time they are wrong. Good odds, wouldn't you say? Anyway, we take you. He will not know. My brothers and I will tell you when a clear day arrives, and he will think we are going fishing, but we will take you and the brothers to see The Forest Isle. It is terrifying but it is beautiful, and you should see it. It will increase your admiration for the work of Almighty God."

Columba thanked him and left him at the Abbey gate. He was stimulated by the prospect of seeing the island.

It was nearly a month later that the son knocked at Columba's door and came in to tell him that the next day would provide the right conditions for the trip to the island. That night, as he and the eight shared their common meal, he told them about it.

They were all curious and wanted to know more about the place and why they were going there. More than one of them signaled for John, who sat next to Columba, to ask him questions. John did as they requested, and Columba told them all he knew about the place, its character, its mythology, the shape of the stone trees, the caves, and the sights of the Scottish coast to be observed from the crest of the stone leaf canopy.

"Going there will be a great buttress to our faith in God's creative powers," he said. "It will give us a greater appreciation of His handiwork. It will give us a chance to rest from our daily labors and maybe return here to the Abbey with renewed energy and dedication to the work God has called us to do."

Satisfied with his explanation, they finished their meal, said final prayers, and retired to bed at sundown so that they would be fresh and strong to make their exciting journey at sunrise.

As the boys had predicted, the morning dawned clear, there was little wind, and from the Abbey the sea looked like glass. After the first service of prayer and breakfast, Columba led his men down to the dock where the boys kept their boats. All four were waiting. There was no sign of the old man.

"We'll take you in three boats," the oldest son said. "Kevin will go fishing as usual, so the old man won't get suspicious."

"You put us where you want us," Columba said.

So they placed three of the monks in each of the three boats making the voyage, in each case a heavy man was told to sit on one side and two lighter men on the other. The boys knew how to balance a boat.

The boys usually rowed out to do their fishing, but since they were going a much longer distance today they had attached their sails. There was just enough wind to power them but not enough to endanger them. The sea remained calm.

The three small boats set out at just after six in the morning, and they reached The Forest Isle at close to midmorning. As they approached it, the monks could see how it had earned its name. It did indeed look like a thick stand of timber carved in stone. The trunks came up out of the sea, and they were topped by what looked like a leafy canopy. The boats passed by the caves and then the trunks that looked like they had fallen toward the water and aimed for what appeared to be the only spot for landing. The water grew choppier as they neared the island, and the boys had to strain every muscle to bring the boats alongside the low level rock where their passengers could alight without damaging their sides.

The monks grew more excited the closer they came to the landing, and by the time the sailors told them it was safe for them to jump out onto the rock their eyes were bright with anticipation. All eight of them, with Columba following, made it safely to the rock, where more than one slipped on the wet surface before getting far enough away from the seafront to find dry walking. When they were all on shore, their robes flapping in the breeze like the wings of large white birds, they looked to Columba for directions.

"This is a free day," he told them with a smile. "You have your bread, your cheese, and your wine. Go exploring. It's a small island. You can't get lost. We will be in no great hurry to go home."

They smiled and nodded and began moving away from him, like children given freedom from a father, their eyes cautiously searching the rocks for the places they wanted to visit. Columba began immediately climbing toward the crest of the leafy top, and he was pleased that no one wanted to follow him too closely. He needed time away from the brothers as much as they needed time away from him.

The remainder of the morning passed peacefully, and Columba ate his meal alone around the time the sun reached its zenith. It was much warmer atop the stone trees, and after he ate he napped on one of the grassy spots that sprinkled the rocky surface. He had no idea how long he had been asleep when a shout of alarm woke him. He sat up and looked all around. He heard the call again, and this time he stood and looked until he saw one of the monks, Brother Bartholomew, waving from the path he had himself taken to the top. He waved back, and Bartholomew finally saw him and rushed forward.

"Father, Father," he said as he reached Columba. He was out of breath, partly from climbing the steep hill to the top, partly from excitement. His face was deep red. "Father," he said, taking a deep breath of the cool damp air, "something terrible has happened."

"What on earth?" Columba said, frightened by Bartholomew's alarm.

"It's Brother John," he said. "He's. . .he's fallen. . ."

"Fallen? How? When? Where?"

"I don't know how or when, but Brother James told me he is lying on a ledge, down in the Cave. He told me to come and get you."

Without another word Columba and Bartholomew started down the narrow pathway off the top of the island, down to the rocks where the three boats lay at anchor. It was slow going because the rocks, especially down near the water line, were damp from ocean spray. All the other monks were gathered there by the jetty, looking toward the walkway that led around the stone tree trunks toward the curve in the forest where the largest of the Caves lay. They turned as Columba and Bartholomew rushed up to them. There was terror in all their faces.

"John. Is he all right? Is he alive?" Columba asked them.

They all shook their heads. No one seemed to know.

"James, you found him?"

Brother James nodded meekly. "I went to look at the Cave, the large one. It was hard going, the ledge is so narrow and wet, but I made it safely. When I got there I saw John, lying at the bottom. I didn't know what to do, so I ran to tell the others and ask for help."

"Was he moving? Did he speak, did he cry out for you to help him?"

"No, Father. He was completely motionless and silent."

"Take me to him," Columba ordered.

Brother James hesitated, obviously averse to the idea of going back over the slick rocks from which at any moment he could fall into the sea, returning to the place where he had seen Brother John lying so still.

"Go on," Columba ordered.

Brother James started up the rocks to the ledge, and Columba followed. Several of the monks fell into line behind them, all of them afraid but curious to know Brother John's fate. About half remained near the boats.

It took them half an hour to make the treacherous journey along the ledge, around the bend in the stone trees, to the Cave. When they got to it there was barely enough room for all of them to stand and peer down toward the slab where Brother John lay motionless.

"My eyes are not as good as some of yours," Columba said. "Can any of you see any sign of life?"

The youngest of the monks, Brother Andrew, holding onto a rock above and behind his head, looked closely for a long time through the hazy light of the Cave, then looked at Columba and shook his head.

"What do you see?" Columba asked him.

"He is not moving, and he appears not to be breathing, and it looks like he has a bad wound on his forehead," Brother Andrew said.

"Let's go down and get him," Columba said.

No one moved. Making the trip along the ledge to this echoing chamber was more than most of the remnant of monks wanted to do. Climbing down the side of the cliff was far beyond the call of duty—or love.

"We'll have to get him with the boat," a voice said from behind the monks. Columba looked toward the voice and saw that the oldest of the blind man's sons had come with them to the scene.

"You can bring a boat around and into the Cave?" he asked the boy.

"We can try. It won't be easy, but that's the only way to get 'im. I know this place. You can't go down there from here, and you sure as hell can't bring him up here and back along that ledge—excuse the language, Father."

Columba looked down again and then nodded. "You're right. And you're a brave man for offering to do this. Let's go back."

They wound their way along the ledge, retracing their hesitant steps, until they all came to the place where the three boats bobbed in the sea. Although Columba showed no anger to the monks who had not made the trek, they lowered their eyes in shame that they have been cowardly. The oldest son talked with his two brothers, and after some minor disputes over logistics, they all three got into one of the boats, the one that looked sturdiest, and set out along the coast line. Columba and his monks waited at the landing rock.

"Did anyone see Brother John after we came on shore?" Columba asked them. He was distraught, but he had a compulsion to talk.

"I saw him for the first hour," Brother Matthew said. "He and I went to the north shore, where the boys told us we could see the nesting birds, the Puffins. But then he wandered off while I stayed to observe them, and I didn't see him again after that."

"Did anyone see him after Brother Matthew?" Columba said.

They all shook their heads.

"Obviously he went to look at the Cave," Columba said. "Someone must have seen him go."

Again they shook their heads.

"Did anyone see anyone else going that way, toward the Cave?"

No one had.

There was nothing more to do, and so they waited. It was more than an hour before the small boat came back around the bend. The three sons brought it alongside the other two boats, and the oldest son looked at Columba and shook his head. The monks gathered around to look at the body lying in the boat.

"Sorry, Father, but he was dead when we got there," the oldest son said.

"Killed by the fall," Columba mused.

"I don't think so, Master. See that gash on his head? It looks like more than something he got from a fall. It's the only such wound on him, aside from the bruises which did come from the fall."

"What do you mean?" Columba said, looking down into the boat at John, seeing the gash. "You think someone hit him?"

"I do. With a rock, it looks like to me."

Columba stared at him, unwilling to believe his ears, and then he sobbed. "This can't be true, not among us, not to this young man, not at the hands of another monk."

The oldest son shrugged. "It's a clean fall from up on the ledge to the rock where we found him. Nothing to hit that would make a deep gash like that."

Columba looked at the three sons. "Did you see him going toward the Cave?" he asked them.

Two of them shook their heads, but one said, "I don't know if it was him, but I did see one of the monks going that way. I thought it was dangerous to do, but I didn't interfere. I thought he knew what he was doing—or that God would protect a fool." He grinned, but Columba scowled at him, and the grin quickly faded away. "But I saw him coming back."

"What?" Columba said with a shock. "You saw him return?"

"Yes, Father."

"Then it wasn't John you saw." He turned to the monks. "Who else went there and returned?"

They all shook their heads.

There was nothing to do but return to Iona. Columba got into the boat with Brother John's body and summoned Brother

Bartholomew to come with him. The other monks divided into two groups of three and got into the other two boats. The three small vessels launched out into the swirling current and headed south and west, toward home.

All the way, for three hours, Columba held Brother John's head in his lap and caressed his hair. He reached out to scoop up sea water and wash the blood away from the wound, but near the gash it was too encrusted to wipe away. Evaporation left traces of salt on John's face, and Columba brushed it away carefully, cautiously, as if not to disturb his sleep. All the way he shed tears for his beloved disciple.

When they reached Iona they found the blind father waiting at the jetty. The old man waited until they had all come to shore. He seemed to know something bad had happened, and he demanded to know what. Columba nodded to the oldest son to tell him the story: the trip to The Forest Isle, which caused the old man's brow to furrow, the discovery of the dead monk's body, which deepened the furrows, and the recovery and return home, which made him give off a disgusted grunt. Then he smiled bitterly.

"I warned him, didn't I, I warned the Master. You heard me."

"You warned me," Columba said. "I heard you."

The old man had not known Columba was standing there. "Forgive me, Master," he said, turning to Columba. "I spoke without thinking."

"It's all right. What you say is true," Columba said. "You warned me, and I didn't listen." He turned to the brothers. "Now we must take Brother John home, to bury him in the church yard, in the ground we have made sacred, the first of our flock to return to the Heavenly Father."

"I am sorry you didn't listen to me, Master," the old man said. "I am more sorry for your loss."

"Thank you."

"Will you come back to see me, soon please, Master?"

"Why?"

"I have something to tell you."

"About the accident?"

The old man shook his head. "It was not an accident, Master. He was killed. A vision is beginning to form in my mind. It is still in a haze, as an island in a morning mist, but it will soon grow clear. Come back to see me."

Columba said nothing. He merely turned and went down to the boat, where the monks were taking up John's body. He followed them as they made their slow journey up the road toward the Abbey. That evening as the sun set over the hill of the Holy Spirit, before they had eaten their evening meal, Columba said mass over Brother John's body.

"He was the best of us," he said in his homily. "He was the purest of heart. He loved all of us, and we all loved him. I loved him." Tears came to his eyes, and he began to weep. The other brothers lowered their eyes. "Forgive me for expressing such personal feelings," he said. "I have said all I can say about him. I now commend his body to the earth and his soul to Jesus Christ. I know that in the Heavenly City he will love and be loved as he was here. There he cannot die."

He bowed his head and let the monks carry the beloved disciple to the newly consecrated land beside the chapel. He followed the procession and watched as they lowered his body into the grave and shoveled dirt over it. He refused food that night, and he kept a modest fast for the next two weeks, until the pain of his loss began slowly to wane.

It was more than two months later, as summer gave way to autumn, before he accepted the fact that he must take seriously what the blind man had said to him. Time and again he brushed away the thought that John had been killed, that one of his brothers would do such a thing. Yet each time he came to pray over John's grave he knew that one day he must face the awful truth that lay always just below the surface of his conscious mind.

VII

My little travel alarm clock woke me at 11:45. I felt like I had just gone to bed, the same way I had felt when awakened by Wes and Ron earlier. Yet adding up the hours before Wes knocked on my door and those since I got to sleep at dawn, I had put in eight hours. It just didn't feel like it. My first thought upon waking was that I had promised Ron MacDonald that I would meet him and be ready to leave at noon. I got up, splashed some water in my face, opted not to shave, and pulled on my jeans and sweat shirt. I found and wore my socks this time, and I took my rain slicker with me.

Although I had slept soundly and been unaware of dreams, my mind had been at work, and I had already arranged a list of questions to ask Kelly on the way to and from Staffa and while there.

The constable and the preacher were waiting for me in the Abbey front yard. "The boat is waiting forrr us," MacDonald said. He handed me a sandwich wrapped in wax paper and a cup of what appeared to be coffee. I thanked him for his consideration. I opened the sandwich and began to eat as we walked toward the jetty. I hadn't realized how hungry I was. It was cold foul of some kind, but man it tasted good.

"Did you sleep any?" Kelly asked me as we walked. He looked tired, hungry, and not at all ready to go on a trip at sea.

"I did actually," I said. "You don't look like you did."

"No," Kelly said. "No sleep at all. I spent the rest of the night and all morning going from room to room, trying to comfort my people. "I only got them all to sleep about an hour ago."

"So they will likely be tucked away while you're gone," I said.

"Yes. I told them not to venture out."

"Did you find out anything more about the. . .death?" I didn't want to call it a killing, and I was pretty sure from what MacDonald had said that it wasn't an accident. Death was the only neutral word for it. I munched my sandwich while he answered.

"Nothing," Kelly said. "No one knows anything—or so they all say. Beth and her husband Tom went their separate ways on the island. He said he felt sea sick and once they were all up on top he lay down in the grass and went to sleep. She went about with Ralph and Julie Harrison for a time, off to the west to look at the Puffins, but then she parted from them without saying where she planned to go. She didn't go back to where Tom was sleeping, or at least she didn't wake him up, because he never saw her again. Patti and Eric Jones saw her going down toward the ledge that led to the Cave but then lost sight of her. Jack and Marilyn Jackson also spent the time apart from each other. They say they have been together too much, were getting on each other's nerves, and decided to spend some time alone. So as you can see I've come up empty."

"Not surprising," I said. I finished the sandwich and took a swig of the coffee. It was plain, no sugar, no cream, and had little taste. British coffee is as bad as British tea is good. I finished it as quickly as I could. "The person who may have harmed Beth would not admit it, and anyone who might have seen what happened would have told about it before you left the island."

"Nobuddy everrr confesses," MacDonald put in. "People today know the law too well. They've seen too many murderrr shows, and they know they'rrre innocent until prrroved guilty. They know if they don't confess it's a hell of a thing t'prrrove guilt, so they clam up."

Kelly and I nodded.

We came to the jetty, where a boat emblazoned with OBAN SPECIAL SERVICES along its side waited for us, and a sailor dressed in a uniform similar to the one MacDonald wore had the motor running. He pulled it forward until it touched the dock, and we scrambled aboard. Despite his girth MacDonald jumped in smoothly; Kelly hopped aboard with the dexterity of a young man who kept fit; and I came on like a sack of potatoes. I tucked the wax paper and empty coffee cup in a garbage can.

The captain made sure we were safely seated and then launched out, making a big circle in the bay and heading north and east. MacDonald took three of the yellow rain slickers with hoods lying to the front of the boat, handed each of us one, and we all three put them on. We knew right away that it was a good idea. The day was overcast, a stiff wind was coming in from the Atlantic, and within a few minutes it began to rain. It was so foggy that we couldn't make out the shape of Staffa until we were halfway across the six miles to her. We stood looking toward our goal, rain pelting us, water dripping off our coats and hoods.

"It'll be a fikkin sarrrry visit," MacDonald said.

"Yes, you're right about that," Kelly agreed.

I wasn't sure that he had understood MacDonald's slang, that he knew he was agreeing to an obscenity, but I didn't comment on it. Wes seemed all too pure of heart to interpret the language.

"We won't staaay long," MacDonald said to me. "All you want to do is see the site wherrre they found the body, am I rrright?"

"Yes," I said. When I nodded, a rivulet of water poured off my head and down onto my chest.

"We'll walk to it arrround the ledge, and you can look down at it," he said. "I can't rrrisk takin' the boat into the cave. The man yesterrrday did it, to get the body, but he had calmer seas. It'd be farrr too dangerrrous in this weatherrr today, you underrrstand?"

"Yes," I said. "So we can't get down to where she was lying from the place where she fell?" I asked him.

"No, it's a sheerrr drrrop. You can't get down without rrriskin injurrry, and you can't brrring someone up it eitherrr."

"I see."

"We'll walk arrround the ledge and look down, and then we'll have t'come back the same way, MacDonald said. "Then I want to talk to Smiley."

"Smiley?"

"He's the crrrazy bastid lives therrre."

"Someone lives on the island?" I said.

"Aye. Crrrazy if you ask me. He worrrks for Herrritage Scotland. Some call 'im Th' Birrrd Man because he loves those Puffins. That's why he volunteerrred for the job. They pay 'im a salarrry, not much, just enough t'get along on. They brrring 'im supplies once a week, he looks out forrr the place, the birrrds mainly but also any visitorrrs who come his way."

"Smiley, you said."

"That's what he's called. Smiley orrr Birrrd Man. Don't know if Smiley's his rrreal name. May be he's called that because he always has a smile on 'is face. He lives in a hut up on top, summerrr, winterrr, yearrr arrround."

"So the island is under government jurisdiction."

"Herrritage Scotland. It's a prrreserve. Was prrrivately owned until the 1970s. The ownerrr, was a rrrich American of Scots descent, he bought it forrr his wife, but then she died and he didn't want it anymorrre, so he donated it to the nation, if we would take carrre of it. One rrrequirement was to have a carrretaker live there, and Smiley showed up to do the job. He got it without competition. No one else wanted it."

We were nearing the island, and the rain came harder, the sea got choppier. The captain slowed the boat to a crawl and came carefully toward the rock ledge that served as a dock. Still we bumped against it with such a shock that all three of us had to brace ourselves to keep from being thrown down. I knew this was going to be an ordeal; but I had requested it; so I knew I had to go through with it.

MacDonald said something too Scottish for me to understand to the captain, who nodded, and then he jumped out of the boat onto the rock ledge. He helped Kelly up and out, and the two of them helped me. The way they treated me made me feel like I was either a child or an elder, in either case in need of great care. I came out onto the ledge and thanked them. "Rrready for an adventurrre?" MacDonald said.

I put on a brave face and assumed a brave voice. "Yes," I assured him, "ready, willing, and I hope able."

Looking up at the rocks I would have to scale, seeing the ledge up there that I would have to follow, noting how it disappeared around the curve in the island, I was not as sure as I pretended to be. In fact my legs felt weak, and my head felt light. I only hoped I wouldn't have one of my ever more regular dizzy spells along the way. I had neglected to take my pill.

We started up, MacDonald leading the way, me following him, Kelly behind me. I figured they kept me between them to catch me if I fell. We got up to the ledge, and I grabbed hold of the railing which I assumed Heritage Scotland had attached to the cliff side. It's a good thing I did because after four steps my feet began to slide on the rain slickened rocks, and without it I would certainly have fallen into the swirling sea below. More and more I doubted the wisdom of coming to view the scene of Beth's death. With every step I called myself a fool. This could be the scene of my death too.

It took the three of us a half hour to go along the ledge, round the curve in the island, and edge our way into Fingal's Cave. As we entered it, the crashing of the waves echoed from the walls.

"This is what inspired Mendelssohn," Pastor Kelly said.

"What?" I asked him.

"Mendelssohn," he said. "He visited this place as a young man, and afterward he wrote an entire concerto about these islands, one part of it about this cave. You can hear the waves crashing as you listen to the music. Hear how this sounds like an orchestra playing?"

"Oh," I said. "Yes." I felt quite ignorant for not having read more about composers. I liked classical music, but I knew little about musicology. "How did you learn about it?" I asked Wes.

"From my flock. You might expect that they know such things. They talked about it coming over yesterday. They all wanted to come here to the cave and listen. The only one who did was Beth. Well, maybe someone else did, but he won't admit it."

We edged forward, further into the cave. At long last Kelly stopped us. "Here's where we saw her body—it was down there," he said, pointing below us, to a flat spot at the bottom, forty feet below where we stood, only a few feet above where the water lapped the rocks.

"She was just lying there?" I said.

"Yes. On herrr back. We could see the wound on herrr forrrehead."

I noted the sheer sides of the cliff leading down to the ledge. She would have fallen straight down, and indeed the only way to recover her body was to come into the cave with the boat.

"Wasn't your sailor reluctant to brave these waves?" I asked him.

"Surrre he was. They werrren't so rrrough yesterday, it was a clearrr day, but they werrre choppy enough to make a landing in herrre dangerous. On the otherrr hand, he had no choice. If we had left herrr body therrre until a rescue boat could have come over, she might have been swept away and neverrr been recoverrred. We went back and told the captain about herrr, and he didn't hesitate. He left us all by the jetty and headed rrright over herrre. He was gone over an hourrr. He came back with herrr body, and we took herrr on shore and bathed herrr head. That took anotherrr hourrr or so. It was almost dark beforrre we set out to returrn to Iona."

Wes nodded that he agreed with the constable's story. I nodded that I understood the details.

I had seen all I needed to see, so I signaled that we could go back. We were turning, exchanging our right hand grip on the guard rail for a left hand grip, ready to head for the dock, preparing ourselves for the hard half hour it would take to reach it, when a voice came booming down on us from above.

"Halllooo," it said.

"What the bloody hell!" MacDonald said.

He looked up, and we looked up with him, and there on the ledge at the top of the cave was a face. It was large and round and gave off a dazzling smile.

"Halllooo," the smiley face repeated. The word echoed through the cave.

"Halloo, Smiley," MacDonald called back and waved an arm at the face.

"Lookin' at the killin' place?" Smiley yelled, still smiling.

"Yes!" MacDonald yelled back.

"I seen it, y'know!" Smiley yelled.

"You did what in hell?"

"I seen it—seen what happened!"

"You, Smiley, stay rrright there!" MacDonald called. "We'rrre comin' up!"

It did take us a half hour to retrace our steps to the dock, and it took us another half hour to get up to the top of the island, where Smiley met us, the big smile still on his face.

MacDonald introduced us, but I noticed that he didn't mention that I was a priest and Kelly was a minister. We were simply Americans who knew the dead woman. That was all the information he gave Smiley.

"You saw it?" MacDonald asked the caretaker.

"Aye," Smiley smiled. Saw the two of 'em arguin' like. They was both wavin' their arms, like this." He demonstrated, gyrating wildly. "I could hear 'em yellin' at each other, but I couldn't unnerstand that they was sayin' like." He paused, lost in thought, recalling the picture.

"Aye. Go on," MacDonald urged him.

"Well, then, this one picked up a rock, not a big one, just one a those you see along the ledge. Shook it at the other one, threatenin' y'know like. The other one threatened back, but without a rock. One without a rock raised her arm, struck out at the other. Then the one with the rock struck back." He demonstrated. "Hit her in the head with it, and she started fallin' backwards. The one dropped the rock and grabbed for the other one, y'know, sort of like tryin' to catch her, but she toppled over and fell, all the way down the cliff, landed on the ledge below, didden move."

"So what did he do then, after she fell?"

"He?"

James T. Baker • Page 72

"The man."

"What man?"

"The one who hit her with the rock."

Smiley smiled. "Wadden a man," he said. "Was a woman."

"A woman?" Kelly and I said simultaneously.

"Aye. Was another woman. Was a cat fight."

"A woman," MacDonald said. "What did she look like?"

Smiley shrugged. "Dunno. Jeans, yellow shirt. Both of 'em was dressed the same way."

"Of course they were," Kelly said. "We all were. We had those shirts done up at home, and we all wore them yesterday. They had " Musical Methodists" printed on the back. And I think we were all in jeans."

"Herrr hairrr?" MacDonald said.

"Hair?"

"Short or long?"

"Short like."

"That's all of our women," Kelly said.

"Colorrr?"

"Brown like."

"That's all three of the survivors," Kelly said. "Beth was the only blond."

"Would you know herrr if you saw herrr up close?" MacDonald said.

"Nooo," Smiley allowed. "She was too far off. She never looked up, she never saw me, an' I never saw her face."

We left Smiley on top of his mountain, to tend to his Puffins, and got back into the swaying boat. Instead of standing out on the deck as we had done on the way over, we got into the cabin and sat down, all three of us in various states of exhaustion. I'm sure I was the worst off, then the constable, then the pastor. It was a matter of age. For a long time, as we bounced over the high waves, no one spoke. We were all processing what we had heard. Finally I looked at Kelly.

"Did you notice anything peculiar about any of the three women, on the way back to Iona, did anyone of them act strange?" I asked him.

"I didn't notice anything unusual. They all three acted upset. They were all three crying. They all three looked after the body, straightened her clothing, kept her protected from the elements. I wasn't looking for strange behavior, I still thought it was an accident, did until the constable here said he thought otherwise, but no, I didn't notice anything unusual about how any of the three survivors acted."

I thought of something else. "You mentioned Beth's husband. His name is Tom, isn't it?"

"Tom Edwards, yes."

"How did he act, you know, when he heard about Beth, when he saw her body, on the way back to Iona?"

"Just the way you saw him in the dining room. In shock. That's how he looked when he heard about it, when he saw her, all the way home afterward. That's how he looked when I got him to bed this morning."

"You said he fell asleep on top of the mountain, that's why he didn't go to Fingal's Cave with Beth?"

"Yes. He was still groggy when we sounded the alarm about Beth. And he acted out of it going home."

"Don't I remember that he missed breakfast?" I said.

"Yes," Kelly said, frowning. "Now you mention it, he did. He overslept. Beth had to go wake him up. He made it to the boat and went with us, but he acted half asleep all the way, then he fell asleep after the climb to the top."

"Does he. . .drink?"

"Drink? Alcohol? Tom? No, no I don't think so. I've never had any hint of it. Certainly he wouldn't drink on this trip. It's a spiritual journey."

I ignored that remark. We Catholics don't separate the spiritual from spirits the way Puritans do. "Could he have been sneaking a snort now and then?"

"It's possible, but I don't think so. Yesterday morning was the first time he acted groggy that way."

My mind was working overtime now. "Pardon me for asking this, Pastor, but have you any indication of a possible. . .physical attraction. . .a romantic attraction. . .between any of the flock, between a man and a woman not married to each other?"

"What? Why, no, not at all. Why do you ask?"

"Well, in my many, many years of living in this world, I have observed that fights between women are usually the result of jealousy, and that jealousy is usually born of rivalry over a man."

"No," Kelly said, frowning, "I don't think that's possible. Beth and. . .no, I don't think so at all." He was silent for a time. "But of course, as we say, the pastor is the last to know." He smiled shyly. "We don't have the Confessional like you Catholics do. We threw that out in the Reformation."

I smiled back at him, to let him know that what I was about to say was meant to be light and friendly. "You Protestants had good reason to be critical of the church back five hundred years ago," I said. "We needed reforming, we needed a good kick in the pants. But I think you may have gone too far. Such as doing away with Confessional. I think there you threw out the baby with the dirty bath water."

Kelly looked at me and for the first time since he came to my room the night before he grinned. The grin turned to laughter. He needed that very badly.

"I think you may be right, Father," he said.

We both had a good laughed. It relieved some of the tension. MacDonald didn't share the humor. He stared at us as if we were both as crazy as Smiley.

Finally back in my room, resting before dinner, weary from the exhausting trip to Staffa, guess Who spoke up.

"I WAS PROUD OF HOW YOU BEHAVED TODAY."

"Oh?" I said. "What part of it?"

"WELL, MAINLY THE QUESTIONS YOU ASKED MISTER KELLY."

"You liked that, eh?"

"CLEVER. AND I APPRECIATE THE WAY YOU SPOKE UP FOR THE CONFESSIONAL."

"Don't mention it."

"IT MIGHT JUST MAKE HIM THINK. THAT'S ALWAYS GOOD FOR THE PROTESTANTS. THEY DON'T DO ENOUGH OF IT."

"If You say so."

"CONFESSION IS GOOD FOR THE SOUL."

"Oh please.

VIII

The thought that kept creeping into Columba's mind all through the autumn and into the winter of that sad year was that one of his seven remaining disciples had likely committed murder, that he had killed his beloved disciple. He despised and scolded himself for doing it, but he kept watching all of the men closely for some hint of guilt. None came. Either the killer had no remorse or he was a very good actor.

Since Columba was the only ordained priest on the island, he was Father Confessor for them all, both his monks and the blind man and his extended family. He listened day after day, week after week to admissions of easily pardonable offenses against the Almighty, without a single lead in his search for the truth. The blind man's sons confessed to lying about weight and cheating fish merchants out of a few coins. Their wives confessed to envy and jealousy when they saw the rich older women come to the island laden in fine clothes and gold and silver trinkets for the Abbey. The monks confessed to taking extra portions of food and neglecting to finish their prayers on nights when they were weary from work in the garden.

All the while Columba was listening to such trivial matters, he mulled over the words of the blind man: he had said he saw a vision forming and that it would grow clearer as time passed. He wondered whether the old man really had clairvoyance, and he wondered whether if he did, the vision was now clear. At long last, with the thought of harboring a homicide still gnawing at him, he went one cold night to the blind man's hut and knocked at the door.

The blind man came and opened to him. "Come in, Master," he said without asking who it was.

"How did you know it was me?" Columba asked him.

"I have my own kind of vision," the old man said. "My hearing, my sense of smell are stronger now that I no longer have sight." He didn't explain whether he recognized the Abbot's walk or his odor or both. "Will you sit down, here by the fire? I can get you a drink."

"Well, perhaps to keep me warm," Columba said. "I'll say yes, to both offers, thank you."

The blind man led him to one of two chairs by the open fire, bade him sit down, and then went to a shelf and pulled down a jug. He filled two mugs with liquid from the jug and brought them to the fire, where he handed one to Columba and sat himself down in the other chair.

"You came to ask about my vision," the man said.

"Uh, yes," Columba said.

He took a sip of the liquid in the mug. It was cold from the shelf and very strong, much stronger than the wine he used in the Eucharist and the beer he let the brothers have with their meals. It burned his throat, and he had to cough to clear it.

"I must tell you, though, as I did when I first came to Iona, that I'm not sure your kind of vision is in accord with Biblical teaching. There is a prohibition against soothsaying."

"Oh, Master, I am not a soothsayer," the man said. "I do not rely on magic potions or consult the occult. I merely let Christ speak to me in visions and report them to the people they concern."

"I see."

"The vision I have about the killing, it will help you to do the work of Christ much better. It will help you to know the truth, and remember that the truth sets a man free."

"So it is written."

Columba waited, but the blind man was silent, sipping his drink, smiling vaguely, his open empty eyes staring toward a dark corner of the room.

"Will you tell me your vision?" Columba said.

"If you want me to."

"Yes. I do."

"Very well," the man said, leaning forward. "You know I was not always blind. The blindness came on to me just a few years before you came here, to rule this island."

"Truly?"

"Truly. When I was a boy, when I was a young man, I had perfect sight. I went to across to Mull and searched up and down the coast of the big island for a wife. I searched the coast because I wanted the daughter of a fisherman, one who could help me survive on Iona. I did not look for the prettiest face, though I rejected several because they were so ugly, but I looked for strength in the arms and legs, someone to help me with my work and give me strong children to help me in my old age. Well, I found her and brought her back." He sighed. "It's a good thing I found her early in life because I needed such a woman later on, when my eyes began to fail. She gave me my four sons, and she took care of me until she died."

"She was gone before I came."

"Oh yes, well before then. She's been gone fifteen year now. But by the time she died the boys could take over. So you see I've been lucky."

"Lucky? But you can't see."

"Oh, that's right. I can't see. And when it first started to happen, when I first began to lose my physical sight, I was in despair. I blamed God for taking away such a precious gift. I feared going into the darkness forever." He leaned closer to Columba, so close that Columba could smell his breath. Now that was indeed an odor. The liquor barely covered the foul stench. "But I learned better. I learned that the more I lost my physical sight, the stronger grew my other sense—and the greater grew my spiritual sight."

"You began to have visions."

"Yes, that's it. At first they were only while I slept, when I was in total darkness, but then they began to appear in the evening, when it was darkest, and finally when I was completely blind they came at all hours of the day and night."

"When did you begin to tell fortunes?"

"Oh, I don't tell fortunes. I simply tell my visitors what I see. I use the gift that God has provided to replace the gift He took away."

"I am told you generally give pessimistic readings."

"Readings? I don't give readings. I tell people what I see in my visions, and if they are pessimistic, as yes they often are, then so be it. I merely warn them of the dire consequences of what they want to do. The desire of most men and women is to do something that will harm them. It is my duty, if they ask me, to warn them about what will happen if they go forward with their plans. If that is pessimistic, let it be."

"You warned us not to go to The Forest Island."

"That's right. I had no concrete vision about it, only a vague outline, but I knew that the chances were great that there would be tragedy."

"I should have heeded you."

"Thank you, Master. That gives me some comfort—but not much. I was terribly sorry to hear about your Brother John. When my son, who stayed behind that day, admitted to me under stern questioning that you had gone ahead with your journey, despite my warning, when I learned that my other three sons had taken you there, I was afraid that something bad would happen to one of my boys. I was relieved to learn that the dead man was not one of them, but I was sorry it had to be anyone. I was especially sorry that it was John, because he was always kind to me."

"He was kind to everyone."

"Yes. But that is the way of the world. It is always the innocent who suffer, always the good who die."

"The world can be cruel. Satan spreads evil all over it."

"Yes." He grunted. "But Master, even evil can give birth to good."

"How so?"

"Well, you don't know the outcome here. Perhaps even the death of this innocent soul can result in a greater good."

"Then you are not a complete pessimist. You do not think things always turn out bad," Columba said.

"No, of course not. I warn people not to take chances, and if they heed my warnings, which many do, they do not suffer. Even those who do not heed me, as you did not, even if there is suffering, sometimes the very suffering can bring better things."

"There is then the hope of redemption."

"Exactly."

Columba sighed. He felt he was ready for the truth. "All right then. Tell me your vision."

The old man sat back in his chair. "It was at first quite blurry, but over the weeks gone by it has become clear. I see two of your monks. One has ventured around the edge of the facing."

"On The Forest Island, you mean."

"Yes, Master. I was often there before I lost my sight. I know it well. I can see the facing and the ledge leading to the Cave. The first monk, who is slightly built, I think it is Brother John, was he small?"

"Yes, quite small. Almost like a girl."

"Yes, that then is John. He has gone alone along the facing, and he makes his way around the bend in the island to the Cave."

"That is true. Why would he do such a dangerous thing?"

"I don't know, Master. All I can do is see the man's body, not look into his soul. That is for men of God, like yourself."

"Yes. Well, go on."

"He enters the cave. He looks up at the sky. He seems to be praying there in that great natural church."

"Yes."

"Now, in a second scene, I see another man, another of the brothers, coming along behind him. The second monk is larger. The small monk turns to face him. Now they are talking. Now they are arguing. They are both waving their arms."

"What are they saying?"

"Master, I cannot hear. The roar of the waves crashing into the Cave is too loud. But they are gesturing angrily at each other. I see the second, the larger brother bending down to pick up a loose rock. He is threatening the smaller man. The smaller man lunges for him, to take the rock, and the other brother hits him in the forehead with it. The smaller man reels backward, toward the precipice. The larger brother drops the rock and reaches out for him, but he falls backward, down the cliff, to the ledge many feet below. The other brother is barely able to keep from following him down. He regains his footing, at the last moment, and backs away from the edge. He hugs himself and begins to bow down. He is shaking. With fear, I think it is."

"How long does he stand there?"

"For many minutes. . .until at last he seems to hear a sound. He rouses himself, he looks all around, and he begins going back the way he came. He disappears around the bend of the island and goes out of my vision."

"Was it then an accident?"

"If you wish to judge it so, Master. The small man lunged at the large man who held the rock, but the large man hit him in the head with it. The large man tried to catch the small man, to keep him from falling, but he fell because he was hit by the rock. I think I would have to call it a killing."

"A killing."

"A killing, not a murder. The man did not intend to kill, but kill he did."

Columba was silent for a long time. It would be his task to determine guilt or innocence, and the blind man made such a decision difficult.

"You know now that the man who fell, the small man hit with the rock, was Brother John," he said. "You do not know who the other man was?"

"I do not know."

"So I am back to the starting point. I have seven suspects."

"Perhaps you do. That I cannot say. Would it help you to have a description of the man's features?"

"What?" Columba started. "Your vision brought you close enough to see his face?"

"Yes. I saw his features. I saw them with my heart. I have never seen the brothers with my eyes. So I do not know which man it was."

Columba held his breath. If the blind man truly had the gift of Vision, he could identify the killer.

"Describe him."

"He had a beard."

"Yes?"

"That is all."

"Nothing more?"

"No. My vision does not take me close enough to see more."

"But. . .that doesn't tell me who the man was. Three of the brothers have beards. Brother John was the smallest of them all."

"If you say so."

"I am down from seven to three, but still. . ."

"That is all I know. That is the limit of my vision."

"I see."

"Except for one thing."

"What?"

"The same man comes each night, after all the other monks have gone to sleep, and prays at Brother John's grave."

"I do that myself."

"I know. I see you as well. You come early. This man comes far later, when everyone else is abed, when he is sure no one will see."

The fire was burning low, and the blind man rose from his chair to find more wood. Columba helped him gather it up and put it in the hearth. He waited until it was burning brightly, warmly, and then he thanked the old man for his service and moved toward the door.

"What will you do?" the blind man said.

"I will seek the Truth in other places, by other means," Columba told him. "I came to you, and you told me some of the

Truth, the part of the Truth that you know. Thank you for doing that. God bless you."

"I am glad to help you, Master," the blind man said. "You seem to believe now that I do have the Gift."

"We shall soon see for sure."

Columba went out of the hut and headed back up the pathway to the Abbey. On the way he met one, then another of the monks, then another, all of them out for the evening walk he recommended they take before retiring. He saluted each as he passed, but the darkness kept him from being completely sure who each one was. No one spoke, and so he couldn't distinguish them by their different voices.

Brother Bartholomew, Brother Peter, Brother Matthew, were the three monks who had beards, and one of them was responsible for Brother John's death. He must find out who it was. The blind man's vision said that it was the one who came to visit the grave in the middle of the monastic night.

Columba stopped at Brother John's grave and bowed his head in prayer. "Dear God in Heaven," he said, "please give me wisdom to know the Truth and to do what the Truth dictates." He looked at Brother John's tombstone, recently carved and set up. It had only his monastic name—his worldly name had been put aside forever—and the date of his death. "I promise you, my Beloved," Columba said softly, "that I will give you Justice and with it the Eternal Peace that you so richly deserve."

He seemed to feel John's presence, bringing with it warmth against the cold night. He stood there for a long time, until the bells signaled the call for final prayers. He would go to the Community service and then to his cell, where he would lie down but would not sleep. He would wait until all but the one other monk were asleep and then return to the graveyard to meet the nightly visitor.

IX

I got back to the Abbey and climbed the stairs to my room just before 3:00. As I got to my hallway I found one of the retreat participants, a man I had met but whose name I could not recall, from Birmingham in England I thought, pushing a cart and taking from it a pot to leave on the small table by my door. There were three other pots not yet delivered, one for each of the other rooms on my floor.

"Ready for your tea?" he said with a smile.

I had found a pot sitting on the little table outside my door both of the last two days, but each day I had touched the pot and found it was cold, and I had left it there to be collected. I like my tea to be either very hot with steam or very cold with ice, not lukewarm.

"This is your assignment for the day?" I asked the man.

"Yes. All week actually. I don't mind, I like doing it. It's one of the easier and more pleasant tasks, bringing people refreshment."

He picked up the pot with a cloth covering his hands and let me take it by the handle. I thanked him and started into my room with it.

"Tea comes every afternoon at this time, doesn't it?" I said.

"Yes. At three." He smiled again and went on down the hallway.

I nodded another thanks and closed my door. I found my cup by the sink and poured the tea. I took it to my bed and sat down and began sipping it.

Tea at three every afternoon, what a good idea, just enough nourishment to help people get through the down time until dinner. As I drank my tea, an idea began to form. That's about as scientific as my approach to homicide ever gets.

I went down to the chapel for what they called Vespers. Beth's body was gone from the altar, and I assumed MacDonald had taken it to the nearest morgue over on Mull. Wes Kelly read the scripture and said a prayer. Then he said: "As you know by now, my flock has suffered a grievous loss. One of our group, Beth Edwards, died yesterday on the Isle of Staffa. As a tribute to her, we would like to offer the following song."

Six of the Kentuckians got up and went to the front of the chapel, to the right of the altar. Tom Edwards remained in his pew. One of them hummed a note, and they began one of the most beautiful renditions of "Abide with Me" I have ever heard. It was obvious that they were excellent musicians with trained voices. Even though I considered "Abide with Me" a "Protestant" hymn, even though I knew that one of the singers had killed the very person to whom the song was dedicated, I was at the end in tears. So were the other participants. Only the singers were stolid and dry eyed as they let the last note die away and trooped slowly back to their seats.

At the dinner that followed I sat at the table with them and observed the women as closely as decency would allow. They ate in silence. They all gave off the same air of shock and sorrow I had seen the day before, the same as the men, with the exception of Tom Edwards whose shock and sorrow were deeper than any of the others and seemed to have grown more debilitating. He was barely able to hold his head up, and he just pecked at his food. I looked closely to see if I could detect that any of the women showed a hint of guilt or fear but found none whatever. Someone was a very good actress. One by one the eight finished their meal, excused themselves, took their trays to the kitchen window, and drifted away. Only Wes Kelly and I remained at the table. After a time the other tables were abandoned as well, and only the people assigned to dish washing for the night were left, working away and talking quietly in the other room.

We sat there for a long time before I broke the silence. "Wes," I said, "I have been giving Beth's death a lot of thought."

"That's why I hired you," he said, then grinned.

I laughed lightly. "The Bird Man says it was one of the women who hit Beth with a rock. He says they were arguing and that she hit her, but he also says she reached out to prevent Beth from falling. We don't know whether the blow to her head or the fall killed her, but in either case the other woman is responsible for her death. She may not have intended to kill Beth, but that was the end result. Do you agree with these assumptions and conclusions?"

"Yes. Yes, I do," he said sadly.

"The reason I asked you about whether there were any signs of a romantic attraction between people not married to each other is that, as I said, I have found the main cause of tension between two women is a man. Tension between two men can be a woman, but it can also be a struggle for power. My suspicion is that the woman who hit Beth thought Beth was stealing her husband's affection and that she wanted to warn her off, that the *contretemps* got out of hand, and that the death was in a real sense an accident. Do you think I could be right?"

"I hope you're right, about the last part. It would be hard going home to telling my congregation that one of our members killed another one; but it would be easier if I can say it was an accident, done in the heat of an argument, unintentionally, even though it proved fatal. People could live with that scenario much easier than with one involving an intentional and premeditated act of homicide."

"I have noticed that none of the three women shows any more remorse or sorrow than the others. They all act exactly the same. Which means that the one responsible is not planning to confess."

"I agree."

"From what Smiley has told us, we know that it was not a simple accident, and for you to say so would be to tell a lie. You must tell your congregation the truth. We could let it go, leave it unsolved, leave the case unresolved; but I think that would be harder on your congregation, knowing that they harbored a killer, than knowing who did it. The one responsible, if we can prove it, will be sent to prison in Britain and will not have to go home for a long time. From what I have read, the sentence for involuntary homicide is lighter here than in the States, but she will likely be looking at several years. Even when she is released, she can settle somewhere other than Lexington. Your church can slowly heal."

Wes scratched his head. "I see what you mean. It's better to solve the crime and let the responsible person come to justice, no matter how painful that might be," he said.

"I think so too," I told him. "Will you help me then?"

"Me? How? I can't go ask each woman if she killed Beth."

"No. That wouldn't do any good anyway. The guilty one is hiding her guilt now, and she would probably not mind lying if asked. No, we have to have proof. I need you to help me break the law in order to uphold the law."

"Break the law? How?"

"Help me trespass. Help me do a search without a warrant."
"How?"

"Are there locks on your doors over at the Center? We don't have them on the doors at the Abbey where I am."

"No. There are no locks on our doors."

"And your names are on your doors, like mine?"
"Yes."

"Okay, good. I'd like you to take your flock for a walk tomorrow morning. Tell them it's to pray by the seaside, to hold a service in memory of Beth. Keep them gone long enough for me to get into their rooms. I need to do a search."

"Will you look for something in particular?"

"Yes. Drugs."

"What? Drugs? Come on. . ."

"Not illegal drugs. Something you can buy over the counter at your local drug store. Sleeping tablets."

"Why?"

"I think there's a connection between Tom oversleeping yesterday morning and his groggy behavior the rest of the day and Beth's death."

"I don't see. . ."

"Can you do it?"

He nodded. "Yes, I suppose so, if you think it'll help solve the crime. I'll stop by their rooms tonight and tell them. When do you want us gone?"

"Take them off after breakfast. Keep them out as long as you can. Since there's no lunch, take them to eat at the café in the village, Adam's place."

"All right."

We stood up and shook hands.

"Father, I am grateful for this," Wes said. "I'm a lucky man to have found you here in this place at this time."

"It seems to be my fate to get caught up in these things," I said.

We parted, and I was in bed before the bells sounded to end the day. I didn't sleep well, despite the fact that I was fully convinced that I knew what I was doing, that I would know tomorrow what I needed to know in order to solve the mystery of Beth's death. Nerves kept me on edge. What I planned to do wasn't exactly breaking and entering, but it was entering without permission. I didn't know Scottish law, but I was pretty sure it was trespassing, and if it that was not a crime, it was at least a transgression.

* * *

I reluctantly ate breakfast with the Kentucky group, hoping the expression on my face wouldn't give away what I was planning, knowing that if I chose another table I might alert them to my intentions. They were still silent, and we exchanged no more than a dozen words over the scrambled eggs, toast, and blood pudding. After we had carried our trays to the kitchen window, I went for a stroll around the graveyard, fingering my rosary, pretending to do my daily prayers, keeping an eye on Fellowship Hall across the road. Around 9:00 I saw Wes come out, and I counted seven followers as they all turned north on the road, heading toward the seaside. If they walked the circle of the island, stopped for a memorial service, and had lunch at Adam's café, they would be gone four hours, plenty of time for me to do my undercover work.

I waited another few minutes, to make sure no one had left something behind and would be returning for it, and then went across to the Hall. It was my first time there, and I noted that it smelled different from the Abbey. It was a new building, no more than ten years old, and it had a fresher odor than the old stone Abbey, not as musty. There were twenty single rooms, each with a name tag on the door in a slot, easily removed and replaced when one individual left and another arrived for a new week.

I went down a hallway, passed rooms of people I knew only slightly. Most of the names brought no faces to mind. I've never been able to remember names. Toward the end of the passage I found rooms for Jack and Marilyn Jackson, then Ralph and Julie Harrison. In the cross hallway were rooms for Patti and Eric Jones, then Tom and Beth Edwards. A wreath hung on Beth's door. The first room in the other hallway that led back toward the front door belonged to Wes. After that were more faceless names. So the American Methodists were grouped together, side by side, all in singles.

I didn't bother to go into Wes' room, but I went into every other one. I was careful, before I entered or left a room, to make sure no one was walking down the hallway. I wanted to be absolutely certain that no one saw the portly Catholic priest committing his misdemeanor. I was surprised at the variety of housekeeping I found. One expects women to be tidier than men, but in a couple of cases the wife's room was messier than the husband's. Eric Jones, for example, was a neatness freak, with his bed made and his clothes carefully hung, while his wife Patti was a complete slob, bed unmade, clothes scattered everywhere, even lying on the floor.

I looked carefully at each person's medicine cabinet, something the rooms in the Abbey did not have. Each of these little cubby holes had a door with a mirror attached to it, while at the Abbey the mirror was attached to the wall and we had to keep our grooming equipment and bottles of medicine along the sides of the sink. It was surprisingly easy to find what I was looking for. The only two who had sleeping pills were Jack Jackson and Beth Edwards (whose things had not been packed up) and in both cases there were two pills missing from the packets. The brands were different, and the pills had different colors. I stole two more from each packet and put them in separate pockets of my jacket, the ones from Jack's in my left, the ones from Beth's in my right.

I went back across to the Abbey and found the cook working in the kitchen. I greeted her and smiled. "Would you by any chance have some tea available for a thirsty man?" I grew up in an Irish neighborhood and knew how to turn on the charm for a Gaelic woman.

She looked at me crossly but then broke into a bright smile. "It's not customarrry to serrrve beverrrages between the meals, except at thrrree o'clock, but forrr a handsome man like y'self, I ca' make an exception."

I flashed my most beguiling grin and said, "Oh, and you are lovely." More of the Gaelic charm.

She laughed and set a cup on the counter and went to the stove, where a pot sat keeping warm. She poured the cup full. "Milk 'n' sugarrr?" she asked me.

"No. I like it straight," I said.

"A man afterrr m'own hearrrt."

We chatted while I drank. She seemed glad to take a break from the cleaning, and she showed great interest in the life of a monk. Scots had not known any monks for five hundred years; and like all lay persons she found it fascinating that a man would forego marriage and children for his religious vocation. She said that without her grandbabies she would feel she had accomplished little in life.

"Oh," I said, "one other thing you have accomplished is the ability to make a grand cup a tea."

She giggled and blushed.

"By the way," I said, as nonchalantly as possible, "you haven't given me any more chores to do. We must all chip in, you know."

"Well, no," she said. "I knew you was busy with th' investigation, so I didn't want to distrrract you frrrom it."

"That's all right," I said. "I'm at a lull in the business. It's time for me to earn my keep. I know. Let me serve the refreshments at three today."

"Oh," she said, "that would be verrry nice. Mr. Baxterrr might like some rrrelief from that. He's been doing it all week. Thank you, Fatherrr."

"My pleasure," I assured her.

I watched from my window as Wes and his people returned to the Hall around 1:00. They all went into the building and presumably to their rooms to rest. At 2:45 I went down to the dining room, where the cook had all the pots of tea or coffee ready, four of them on a tray to take up to the abbey rooms, twenty of them on a pushcart to take across to Fellowship Hall. She also gave me a list of which participants got tea and which got coffee.

I delivered the four to the abbey rooms first, my own included, although I suspected my tea would be cold before I returned for it. Then I pushed the cart across the road and into Fellowship Hall. Before I started my deliveries I put two of the pots, both coffee, aside for Tom Edwards and Marilyn Jackson and dropped the two sleeping tablets from Jack Jackson's medicine cabinet into Marilyn's pot and the two from Beth's cabinet into Tom's pot. Then I delivered each pot to the table at the appropriate door. I was scared senseless, and I didn't stop shaking until I finished the whole delivery and had the push cart back to the kitchen. Then, still nervous, I went to my room and waited for results.

Just before 5:30 the bells rang for Vespers, and I got dressed and went down. I watched as the participants filed in. The Kentuckians were slow arriving, apparently still tired from their long walk around the island. I kept a close watch on them and counted them off as they entered the chapel. Ralph and Julie Harrison came in with Wes Kelly. I was pleased to see that they were smiling at something one of them had said. I thought perhaps they were beginning to shake the pall. Patti and Eric Jones, slob and neatnik, followed in a minute or two. They weren't smiling, but they were not dragging, which meant that at least they had shed some of their sense of mourning. That made five of the eight survivors. Then just before the service began I saw Jack Jackson enter the back door, and following behind him, expressionless but as wide awake as anyone in the building, came his wife Marilyn. They sat in the same pew but some distance apart. I didn't expect to see Tom Edwards, and he didn't come.

At the dinner table Tom's name came up, but no one showed undue concern. Wes allowed that he was probably tired from the walk, as they all were, and that he likely didn't feel like company in his grief.

"Where is Beth?" I asked him, being purposely provocative, looking over the faces at the table for some kind of reaction. None came.

"They took her to Oban," Wes said. "There's no mortuary on Mull. And Oban has the nearest forensics lab." He lowered his voice so that only people at our table could hear him. "They won't give us leave to have a funeral service until all matters are settled." He hesitated before going on. "I don't think Tom wants a funeral service here anyway. I think he prefers to take her back to Kentucky and have a graveside there."

I nodded. "Makes sense." I've noticed that Protestants, since they don't have funeral masses, seem content to have simple services in cemeteries.

"It's all so. . .disconcerting," Wes said. "Not knowing when we can leave." Several of the others agreed.

I commiserated but then finished my meal as hurriedly as I could and excused myself. I took my plate to the kitchen window and left the dining room.

I made myself walk slowly as I left the abbey and crossed the road to Fellowship Hall. I went down the hallway to Marilyn's room and picked up the coffee pot. It was light, obviously empty. I went to Tom's room and lifted his pot, and it too was empty. They had both taken their sleeping potions.

I knocked lightly at Tom's door, but there was no response. I knocked again, and still nothing. I turned the knob and pushed the door open. The light was off, but there was still sufficient daylight coming through the window to see clearly. Tom lay on his back, the comforter pulled up to his chest, fast asleep. He was snoring softly.

I went over to him and touched him on the shoulder. "Tom?" I said. He didn't respond. I took his arm and raised it, then shook it. "Tom?"

He roused and stared at me through bleary eyes. "What?" he said with a yawn. "What's the matter?"

"It's Father Columba," I said, turning loose of his arm, which fell to his side.

"Father?" he said, blinking to focus his eyes.

"Yes. You seem to have overslept."

Tom struggled and made himself pull up in bed so that he was sitting back against the headboard. "What time is it?" he asked.

"You're missing supper."

"Oh. Well, that's all right. I don't have much appetite anyway."

"How do you feel?"

"Like I've been drugged," he said, rubbing his eyes with the balls of his hands. "Real groggy."

"Like you felt when you went to Staffa?"

"Yes. Exactly. I overslept then too, and I was ga-ga all day."

"What do you think it is?"

"I don't know. I thought I was over the jet lag, but apparently I've still got it. Man, my head hurts."

"Well, you just rest," I told him. "You'll likely sleep the rest of the night, and you'll be back to normal in the morning."

"You think?"

"I'm sure of it."

I helped him slide back under the comforter and waited until he fell back to sleep. Then I left the room and closed the door.

I smiled as I went down the hallway. As I was leaving the building, the Kentuckians were returning. All of them were talking, including Marilyn Jackson. I told them I had checked on Tom and that he had made an early night of it. They all took my word for it.

"Wes," I said, "may I talk with you?"

He stayed behind, and we went out into the road.

"I know now what happened."

"You do?"

"Yes. I'd like to meet with your people tomorrow morning, say at ten o'clock, in the chapel."

"All right."

"Do you know how I can reach MacDonald?"

"He hangs out at the café. He was there at noon."

I thanked him and let him go to his room. I walked down the road to Adam's place and went inside. MacDonald sat at a table, nurturing a cup of tea. He looked up at me with a skeptical air.

"So what do you know, Fatherrr?" he said.

"More than I did. I know who hit Beth with the rock. I know why."

"You gonna tell me?"

"In time."

"All rrright," he said. But y'do know everrrything, rrright?"

"Right."

"Ya have prrroof."

"Yes."

"So what do we do?"

"We meet with the Kentuckians in the chapel at ten tomorrow morning. Have your boat and captain waiting at the jetty. I think you'll be able to take someone to Oban for questioning."

"It's a deal." He grinned. "I had no idea how t'solve this thing. How did you do it?"

"I muddle through, but I do seem to have a knack."

"That y'do, Fatherrr Columba. You work mirrracles. Like your namesake."

"Oh no," I told him. "I don't work miracles."

On my way back to my room, I was called on that.

"WHAT'S THIS ABOUT MIRACLES?"

"I just said I'm not a miracle worker. I was being humble, as usual."

"YOU'RE PROUD OF YOUR HUMILITY, AREN'T YOU?"

"I guess I am. What are You proud of?"

"HAVING MADE YOU HUMBLE. ON THE OTHER HAND I DIDN'T MEAN FOR YOU TO BE SO AWARE OF IT."

"I'm tired."

"GET YOUR REST. YOU'LL NEED IT."

"I know."

X

Father Columba waited in his cell until all was quiet, and then he waited another hour before he went outside and made his way to the wall that the monks had built to enclose the ground made sacred to house the dead. Only one grave lay inside the yard, that of Brother John, and it was the focus of Columba's attention that night. He did not go through the gap where he planned to have a gate placed at some time in the future, but rather went down the wall to a spot where he was not likely to be seen by anyone approaching. He sat down on the ground. The earth was hard with cold and covered with frost. His robe was made of wool, but he could feel the frost coming through it. He hoped he wouldn't have to sit there long.

He got his wish. He had only been there a few minutes when he saw a light. The Abbey door was ajar, and someone was coming out into the yard with a lantern. Since each monk had a chamber pot in his cell, it would not be someone coming out to relieve himself. He watched the light, flickering in the light breeze, as it came toward him and passed through the gap. He stood up and watched the light go to Brother John's grave. There it stopped and settled uncertainly to the ground, like a bird unsure of the terrain where it was landing. Columba knew that he had discovered John's nightly visitor, the monk with the beard which the blind man had seen in his vision.

Columba eased down along the wall, went through the gap, and walked softly toward the light. His steps crackled in the frost, but the person who had brought the light showed no sign of hearing him. When he was close enough he saw a monk kneeling on both knees in front of the gravestone, beside the lantern. He waited for a moment and then cleared his throat. The monk jumped, let out a soft cry, and stood up and turned to face him. Columba saw the beard, and he knew the blind man's vision had been true. Then he made out the monk's features: it was Brother Peter.

"Master," Peter said, "what are you doing here?" His voice, which was usually a baritone, was high and strained.

"I should be asking *you* that question, Brother Peter. What are *you* doing here, in this place, at this time of night?"

"I am. . .I am praying for Brother John's soul, that he might go peacefully and quickly into the presence of God."

"Yes, we all pray that this may be," Columba said. "But why do you come each night at this hour?"

Peter looked surprised. "How do you know that I come each night?"

"A revelation," Columba said. Then he realized that this statement would simply add to the list of spiritual powers people were adding to his account, and so he went on. "A revelation—from another."

"Old Adam," Peter said with a resigned sigh. "He sees all kinds of things in his darkness."

"It seems so."

"He told you he saw me here nights?"

"Brother Peter," Columba said, "do *you* need to tell me something? Do *you* need to confess something to God?"

Peter hesitated for a moment but then shook his head vigorously. "No, Father, no, I do not."

"Are you sure?" Columba pressed him. He felt he couldn't let the man off this easily. "To lie to God is to put your soul in mortal danger." Peter said nothing. "Your body will perish, but your soul will live forever. You do not want to risk its eternal salvation by lying before God."

Peter kept his tongue, and Columba waited. At last he caught his breath and gave out a sob. "Please, Father, leave me alone."

"Do you have a confession to make?" Columba insisted.

Peter's chin dropped. He nodded. "Yes, Father, yes I have something to say—to you—to God."

"Good," Columba nodded. He leaned over and picked up the lantern and put his arm around Peter. "Let's go to my cell. God wants the truth, but He doesn't want us to freeze to death."

Peter nodded and laughed through his tears. "Yes, Father," he said.

The two of them went through the gap, made their way into the Abbey, and came to Columba's cell. Columba put the lantern on his writing table, and the two men sat down in chairs facing each other.

"Father, forgive me, for I have sinned," Peter said.

"How, Peter? What have you done that needs forgiving?"

"I have lied. I have sinned, a most terrible sin, and then covered up my sin with lies, and therefore I have compounded the sin."

"Sin? What sin?"

"I am. . .responsible for Brother John's death."

So it was true, it was confirmed. Columba sat back and looked at Brother Peter, whose face showed pure anguish. "You killed him?"

"No, Father. I didn't. At least I don't think so, not directly, and certainly not on purpose. But had it not been for me, for my weakness, for the jealousy that consumed me, for the anger my jealousy fueled, he would not be dead now. I lied when I said I knew nothing about his death. Oh Father, I have committed the unpardonable sin."

"We must let God decide that, Peter," Columba said. "No one is quite sure what it is."

"I know what it is, and I have committed it."

"Well, don't be too hasty. . ."

"Father, it has been weeks now. I have had time to think it over, and I am sure what I have done cannot be forgiven."

Columba was struck by the hopelessness he heard in Peter's voice. He felt constrained to tell Brother Peter something no one else in the community knew, hoping that it would save him from despair. "I myself have taken human life, Peter, and I have given commands that led to the deaths of many more than I myself killed personally. This was in time of war, that is true, but they were human lives nonetheless, and I was to blame for their deaths. I believed I could never atone for what I had done, but God in His grace made me see things differently. I turned to Him with a contrite heart, I threw myself on His mercy, and He heard my plea."

Columba reached out and touched Peter on his knee. "God forgave me, He opened a door to a new life for me, and He brought me to this place and to this life in order to atone for what I did."

Peter's eyes brightened. He looked questioningly at his Master. "Do you think, in my case. . ."

Columba sat back. "Tell me what happened," he said with a reassuring tone of voice.

Peter wiped his eyes and took a deep breath.

"I was jealous, Father, jealous of Brother John." He stopped and looked away, into empty space.

"Jealous?"

"Yes, jealous. Jealous of his place always next to you, eating, taking walks. Jealous that he was your favorite and I was just one of the brothers. Jealous that you loved him more than me and jealous that he loved you more than me."

"I see," Columba nodded, an ache forming in his stomach. What he had feared was apparently true. He had shown favoritism, and it had caused conflict among his followers.

"I was your first disciple."

"Yes, that's true, you were.

"He was so fair, so kind, so loving, that I knew it was only natural that you would love him more than the rest of us, that he would be first and I would be second; but still it drove me mad. The fact that he loved you more than he loved me made it even worse. The two men that I wanted most to please, that I wanted to love me, were closer to each other than either one was to me."

"How long did this fester in you, Peter, this jealousy, this anger?"

"So long that I can't remember when it began. It grew hotter slowly but surely, and at last that day it reached the boiling point."

"On The Forest Island."

"Yes. So long as we were here, on Iona, I kept my feelings inside me. I followed the routine, I worked, I prayed, I ate and slept by the rule. I was able to push my vicious thoughts aside. Going away, to another place, escaping for the moment the habits that kept them locked up let them loose. They were demons that went howling and shrieking out of me, only to circle and come back to light on me. They settled in my muscles and led me to violence."

He paused, calling himself back to his narrative. "That day on The Forest Isle, I saw John going off by himself, and I followed him. I don't know what I intended to do with him, perhaps to talk to him, to tell him how I felt about him, to warn him not to take advantage of your preference for him, I don't know. I didn't know where he was going, but I wanted to meet with him, just the two of us, and have it out.

"I didn't care what he would think. I didn't care what he would do. He might go to you and tell you what I said, how I felt, and I might have to leave the Community, but I could keep my feelings to myself no longer. I followed him as he went up that slick rocky pathway, around the bend in the island, and into the Cave. With the roar of the waves, the echoes inside the Cave, he didn't hear me or see me until I called his name.

"He turned and smiled at me; but the smile was not one of love or even friendship, it was a mocking smile. At that moment my love turned to hatred, and I wanted to hurt him. Yet all I did was make threats. I did not tell him how I felt about him, I just told him that he was making a fool of himself by sitting next to you at every meal and sopping up your affection. I quoted the Scriptures: 'The first shall be last and the last first.' I told him that he was reaping his reward here on earth and would not have one in heaven. My words did no good. He didn't take them to heart. He laughed at me."

Peter sobbed and dropped his eyes, then his head.

Columba reached out and touched him on the shoulder and coaxed him to look up. He smiled at him and gestured for him to go on talking.

"The more I said, the more he laughed, and the more angry I became. Before I knew it I was shouting at him. I don't remember what I said, but I must have insulted him because after a time he began shouting back. I saw his smile, that nasty, disdainful smile fade, to be replaced by a twisted snarl. He was as angry as I was. We were both shouting, and our voices were as loud as the beating of the waves. Then he made a fist and raised his arm and came toward me. I did the same to him. He struck me, and I struck him. He backed away and I reached down and picked up a rock, just to protect myself, I had no thought of using it. But he came at me again, and I struck him. But as God is my witness, Father, I struck him in self defense. I didn't mean to hurt him, I just wanted to ward off his attack. I wanted to stop him coming at me. I was surprised and terrified when I saw blood on his face and then the jagged crease in his forehead where the rock hit him. I backed away, toward the Cave's wall, just trying to avoid a counter attack."

Peter sobbed.

"The blow to his head did stop him coming at me, but then something worse happened: he began to reel backward. He was near the edge of the ledge, and suddenly I was afraid he might fall. I lunged forward, to grab him, to keep him from falling, but he saw me coming and backed up further. That's how I know he was alive then, that the blow had not felled him. Before I could reach him, he stepped back too far and went over the precipice. I screamed out in horror and ran to the edge and watched him hit the flat place below with a mighty jolt. I called to him, but he made no response. He moved once, he was still alive when he hit bottom, but then he was still."

Peter sobbed again.

"I waited for a long time, hoping he would revive, and when he did not I hurried back along the ledge, around the bend, and up the hill to where the other monks were lolling about on top of the island. I came first to Brother James, and as calmly as I was able to act and sound I asked him if he had seen Brother John. He said

Good for the Soul • Page 101

he had not. He didn't ask me why I wanted him. I told him I had seen John going along the ledge, toward the Cave, and wondered if that were wise. James looked worried. He asked if I thought he should go and see about him, and I said perhaps it would be a good idea. Later in his excitement at finding John's body James didn't remember that it was me who put him onto John's scent, and of course I never mentioned it to anyone. When you asked us if anyone knew anything about John's trip to the Cave, I lied and denied knowing anything."

Peter's story was over. Columba watched him closely, and he noted that as soon as he stopped talking his brow grew smooth and his eyes cleared. The confession had brought him a measure of peace.

"God will never forgive me," Peter said firmly.

"You have confessed—to me whom you can see—to God who while invisible is as much here as I am," Columba said. "That is all you can do. I will do all I can do. God will do the rest."

He rose and coaxed Peter to rise and stand with him. He looked deeply into Peter's eyes. "You will have to go away," he said.

"That will do no good, Father. Wherever I go, my shame will follow me."

"No. Your story will never leave this room. Only you and I and God will ever know. You will begin a new life, the way I did when I left Eire and came to live on Iona."

"Where can I go?"

"You must go to a foreign land."

"A foreign land?"

"Like Cain."

"Like Cain?"

"Like Cain. He killed his brother, as you did. He went away into a foreign land, he made a new start. I followed Cain's example, and now so must you. You will go to Mull, cross into the land of the Scutti, and then go south, among the Saxons, the barbarians who have invaded the south of Britain."

Peter shook his head. "I have heard bad things about them, Father. I have heard that they are violent, that they kill strangers, especially those who try to teach them new ways."

"Yes, that is true. It will take courage. You will be like Saul of Tarsus, who became the Apostle Paul, who risked death throughout his life in order to take the Gospel to the ends of the earth."

Peter nodded. "It is what I deserve. It is a just sentence."

"It will be both your punishment and your salvation. No matter what happens to you among the Saxons, you will find atonement."

Peter nodded, and then he smiled. "A new life," he said.

"A new life."

"I will go at once."

Columba walked with Peter back to his cell. "Today is midweek. The blind man's sons will go to Mull at sunrise, to take him for his Readings and to bring the pilgrims over to me. You will ride with them. Once you are on Mull you will make your own way. You will take nothing with you. You will eat the food and stay in the homes of people you meet. You will follow the directions of those who know the countryside. At a certain point you will turn south and go into the lands that are now under the command of the Saxons."

Peter nodded.

"We are both sinners, Brother Peter," Columba said. "It is my penance to stay here, when I would like to go. It is your penance to go, when you would like to stay here."

* * *

Neither Peter nor Columba slept, and before the other monks came down at daybreak they met in the dining room to share bread and wine. Then they walked together to the landing. It was the longest walk Columba had taken since the morning he left his Abbey in Ireland so many years before.

The blind man and his sons were already in the boat, preparing to launch. Columba called to them and raised an arm for them to wait. The blind man looked toward him.

"Master," he said with a smile, "I have been expecting you."

"I'm sure you have," Columba said with a smile of his own.

"I saw you last night in my dreams. You were coming from the Abbey down to the sea side. A brother came with you."

"He is here," Columba said. "Men, Brother Peter needs a ride with you across the strait. I am sending him on a mission for the Community. You need not wait for him this afternoon. He will not be returning. He will be gone for a long time."

The sons nodded their assent. The old blind father smiled. "So," he said, "you have found the truth, have you, Master?"

"Yes," Columba said. "We have found the truth, and it has set us free."

"Had a long night, did ye?"

"No. Actually it was a short night. It went very fast."

The old man slapped his legs and howled with laughter and ordered his sons to get busy with the craft. "Time to go," he yelled, still laughing. "Come on then, brother," he said in the direction of Columba's voice.

Brother Peter stepped aboard the boat, wearing his simple habit, with open toed sandals despite the cold weather, no knapsack, not a single worldly possession. He took a seat next to the blind man, looked toward the far shore, looked back again, and raised a hand of farewell to Columba.

"God be with you, Brother Peter," Columba called as the boat slid out into the water.

Columba watched for a half hour as the boys guided the boat to the other shore. By the time it reached the opposite side he could no longer make out individuals. Brother Peter was gone— to his fate.

XI

I did not go to breakfast the next morning, I followed the Biblical injunction to fast and pray, and so I do not know how many of the Kentuckians ate. The first I saw of them was when they came into the chapel at 10:00. They all moved slowly, tentatively, not knowing what was coming, fearing the unknown. Despite what I knew—or was pretty sure I knew—I still could not have told by their demeanor who was and who was not guilty. Constable Ron MacDonald stood at the back door, pointing each one toward the front rows, and when all eight were there he closed and locked the entrance. This was a matter only for the people involved. They alone had been on Staffa on Tuesday.

Without warning the words to the old song "Frankie and Johnny" came to my mind: Ten men are goin' to the graveyard, but only 'leven are acomin' back." There were ten of us in the room, and if I was right in my calculations, one of them would not be going home any time soon.

I looked the group over. The Kentuckians sat on the front four pews, all near the aisle, while MacDonald stood back a bit in the aisle, his arms crossed over his chest, looking very officious. I cleared my throat.

"Before I start," I said, "does anyone have anything to add to what you have said before? There is still time for new revelations. There is still time for a confession."

I waited and looked each person in the eyes. Not a single hint of any new facts or any recognition of responsibility.

"All right then," I said. "I want to say that I am an amateur at this. Pastor Kelly has faith in my deductive ability because of things he has read in the press, but I make no such claim to any superior talent in the field of investigation. I just follow hunches, and I'm wrong about as often as I'm right, but somehow I seem to wade through swamps of lies to the truth."

There was still no response. The guilty and innocent alike were waiting for me to tell them what I thought. It reminded me of the history classes I had taught for such a long time. I was the authority. I was supposed to reveal the truth. I was being paid to tell them what they should know. They would let me do all the work. I quickly buried those memories of educational frustration and went on.

"All right then," I repeated myself, "here is what I have deduced. In this room there are ten people, and eight of them are innocent, at least innocent of the death of Beth Edwards." For the first time there was a gentle stirring among the Kentuckians. "Four of the eight are Pastor Kelly, Beth's husband Tom, and of course Constable MacDonald and myself, since we were not on Staffa with you." There was another gentle stirring. "After deliberation, I have eliminated from consideration four others." I looked down at the Harrisons. "Ralph, Julie, you are in the clear." I looked over at the Joneses. "Patti and Eric, so are you."

This time the stirring was more pronounced. Everyone there knew that I had not eliminated Jack and Marilyn Jackson. Eight pairs of eyes fluttered their way without settling on them. The two of them blushed, the first emotion I had seen from either one, but neither said a word. They just sat staring at me.

"So in this grizzly mess, there are three guilty parties," I said.

For a moment no one spoke. I could see eyes flashing around the room and could almost hear the mental gears turning. Only Wes Kelly found a way to speak up. "But F-father," he stuttered. "If you have eliminated eight and there are only ten of us here, how can there be three guilty people?"

I sighed. "One of the three guilty ones is dead."

"Beth? She is guilty. . .of her own death?"

"In a sense she is. Her behavior, I believe, led to the confrontation that in turn led to her death," I said.

"But how. . ."

"Let me explain my reasoning," I said. I felt just the least bit dizzy. It crossed my mind that I had forgotten to take my blood pressure pill again. That meant I had not taken it for two days. That was a dangerous risk since this session was sure to increase my blood flow. I took a step or two, back and forth before the altar, to calm my nerves and make my head stop spinning. Walking seemed to help.

"The only objective eye witness to Beth's death is a caretaker on Staffa." Marilyn started, her eyes enlarged. "His name is Smiley, at least I think it is; he is called the Bird Man, and he is a queer duck; but he has a keen eye, and he told me he saw what happened." Now Marilyn looked distressed. "He said there was an argument, between Beth and another person, that the other person struck Beth with a rock, that Beth fell backward, that the other person reached to stop her from falling, that in the confusion she fell over the precipice."

I let the story sink in. I particularly emphasized the way the "other person" reached for her, in order to give every possible nuance to the possibility of innocence, hoping that this would smooth the way toward an admission.

"Now that left, when he first told the story, eight possible candidates. But then he shocked me with a final revelation. The 'other person' in the struggle was a woman. That of course reduced the number to three."

Someone sighed, but I couldn't tell who it was. I looked at Jack and Marilyn, there was no need to hide the truth now, but they still sat stone faced.

"Three women in addition to Beth were on the island. Smiley was way up on the top of the mountain, too far to see any details of facial features, and the jeans and shirt he said she was wearing matched that of all the visitors to the island, men and women alike."

Once again I paused and took a few steps. That was not to increase the drama so much as to clear my head. The dizziness continued.

"This led me to give the whole story deeper consideration. What could have led two good Methodist women, both church musicians, to have an argument, an argument so heated that one would strike the other with a rock and despite trying to keep her from falling, caused her death? I concluded that it must have been the old, old story. Why do women fight? Jealousy. What makes one woman jealous of the other? A man. So the argument must have been caused by one woman's jealousy of the other over the affections of a man."

I couldn't really tell them how my mind jumped to the next step in the inquiry. I'm not a Dominican. I don't always follow pure logic. I get hunches, and God alone knows where they come from. The next step came on a hunch. Maybe it was something in the tea I was drinking.

"I thought then about Beth's husband Tom and how he had overslept the morning of the outing and acted groggy all day. He fell asleep in the grass on top of the island. Why? I wondered if that had something to do with his wife's death. Not a strictly logical step forward, but why not? So I engaged your pastor in a bit of illegal snooping."

I looked at Wes and he blushed. I looked at Constable MacDonald, and he frowned. I knew we had done something wrong, but I hoped that the good we had accomplished might override the bad and that Wes and I wouldn't be given a day or two in jail or a fine.

"You will remember that your pastor took you on a long morning walk yesterday and that at the seaside he held a memorial for Beth. Well, during the time you were gone I searched all of your rooms, including Beth's. I didn't go through your personal effects, your underwear and such, I'm not a pervert, and I knew exactly what I was looking for.

"I was looking for sleeping pills, and I found two sets, each set in those little packets you punch out, one belonging to a woman, one to a man. The woman was Beth." I let the information sink in. "The man was you, Jack." I looked at him and saw a pained expression on his face. I knew then for sure that he was guilty.

"There were two pills missing from Beth's packet," I said, "meaning that she had either taken them herself or given them to

Tom. Since Tom had overslept and been groggy all day, I concluded she had given them to him the night before."

I took another few steps. My head was spinning again. I had to remember to take my medicine.

"There were also two pills missing from Jack's packet, but since neither he nor Marilyn showed signs of being drugged, I had to think of an explanation. So I took two more pills from each packet, careful to remember which came from which—which wasn't hard because they were different colors—and yesterday afternoon I volunteered to put out the tea and coffee. I put the two pills from Marilyn's packet in Tom's pot and the two from Jack's in Marilyn's pot. Then I waited to see what would happen.

"Tom again overslept, missed Vespers and dinner, and I had to go to his room and shake him awake. He was so groggy that he declined dinner and stayed in bed. On the other hand, Marilyn was wide awake at Vespers and at dinner and showed no effects of the pills."

"Why was that?" Constable MacDonald said.

"To me it means that either the pills Jack gave Marilyn are duds—or that Marilyn has an immunity, a resistance to them. They didn't affect her last night, and apparently they didn't affect her the night before Staffa."

"Strrrange," MacDonald said.

"Yes. But the import of it all, I think, is that Jack's attempt to make Marilyn sleep failed, while Beth's attempt to put Tom under succeeded. Why would they want their partners to sleep soundly through the night? They were in single rooms, but they couldn't risk husband and wife knowing that they were going to meet."

Jack Jackson gave way at last. He dropped his head and held up his hands. "All right," he said. "Let me explain. This is all my fault." He looked up, and the façade he had kept intact to this point broke. His face was twisted with embarrassment and shame. "Marilyn may have killed Beth. . ."

"What?" Marilyn Jackson shouted, standing up from her pew and glaring down at her husband. Her façade was gone too. "I did not kill Beth. It was. . ."

"It was an accident, I know," Jack said. "You've told me that. But what I'm trying to say is that, regardless of what happened in the Cave, it's my fault—and it's Beth's. We. . .sinned."

"Yes, you sinned," Marilyn shouted at him. "You broke your vows. You yielded to temptation, you betrayed me and Tom. May God damn you—to hell!" She burst into tears.

Wes Kelly went across the aisle and put his arms around Marilyn and brought her across to sit beside him. She put her head on his shoulder and continued to cry.

"It's been going on for weeks," Jack said as soon as she was an aisle away from him. "Beth and me. It was all in our minds when we were back home, but it was adultery nonetheless. 'If you think to do it in your heart, you've done it in reality,' so says the Bible."

I didn't correct his quotation. It sounded a bit off, but for all I knew he might be quoting one of those new translations Protestants use.

"I don't know, but being here on this island, it was different from being at home, and the longer we were here, that whole first week, our desire for each other continued to grow. Finally we agreed that on Saturday when we went into town we would buy the sleeping tablets, to be sure Tom and Marilyn didn't know, and meet secretly. God help me, we did. I went to her room Monday night, and Marilyn found out."

"Marilyn found out," I said, "because her pills didn't work."

"They didn't, but it would have been better if they had," Marilyn said, her voice thick with mucous. She stood up, and Wes stood up beside her. "I heard him leave his room. I thought he was going down to the toilet, but when he didn't come back for so long I thought he might be sick. Silly me, I cared about him, I wanted to see if he was all right, and if not to see if I could help. I went to the men's washroom and knocked, but there was no answer. I went in, and no one was there. Then I heard sounds, they were coming from Beth's room, sounds that so disgusted me I could hardly keep from throwing up. I went to the end of the hall, by the window, and waited in the shadows, and after an hour he came out of her room and went back to his own. That's when I knew for sure."

"You confronted her the next day on Staffa," I said.

"Yes. I only meant to warn her off. But when I told her I knew—I didn't mince words, I told her I knew she was after my husband—she got furious. She denied it at first, but I told her what I had seen and heard. Then she got even more angry. She threatened me, honestly that is what happened. She said she would kill me. She called me a whore. I picked up a rock, just to defend myself, that is the truth, I felt I was in danger, and when she came at me I hit her. I only meant to make her back off, but I hit her in the forehead. She reeled back, the way you said, and I tried to catch her, the way you said, the way the man at the top saw it, but she cowered back from me, blood flowing down from her head, and she fell over the edge and down to the rocks below."

Marilyn began to sway, then to fall, and Wes Kelly was barely able to keep her from sinking to the stone floor. She didn't lose consciousness, but she had to cling to Wes to keep from collapsing. Wes himself looked distressed. I wasn't sure whether it was because of the killing, the adultery, or the language being used. Maybe it was all three.

Constable MacDonald came down the aisle, and for a moment I thought he looked like a celebrant coming to the altar for bread and wine; but then I realized that he was coming to do his secular duty. He came up to the pew where Kelly held Marilyn in his embrace.

"I'll have to take herrr to Glasgow," he said to Kelly.

"Can you give her time to pack?" Kelly said.

"I guess so," MacDonald agreed and backed away. Then he said, "If all a ye want t'go, I'll orderrr a helicopterrr larrrge enough for ye all."

"Yes, do," Wes said. "We all want to go home."

"Not me," Jack said. He was standing up now, facing his wife. "I'll go with you to Glasgow, but I'll be staying with her."

MacDonald frowned. "Well, sirrr, that could be a long time. "If it's found t'be manslaughterrr—we call it that even if it's a woman that's killed—even without intent, that's usually five to seven yearrrs."

"I don't care."

"Suit yourrrself. All the rrrest of you can go home to Amerrrica. I'll arrrange the trrransporrrtation for you about midafterrrnoon."

MacDonald led us out of the chapel. Other guests stood in the Abbey garden watching. The Kentuckians followed Wes across the road to Fellowship Hall, to pack their things and prepare for the long trip home. Only the Jacksons would not fly home.

*　*　*

I went down to Adam's café for lunch, which was a fish sandwich. I dined at a table by myself. Some of the other retreatants were there, but I preferred not to talk with them. They would get the story about Marilyn's arrest from hearsay, and what they got would be wrong, but I didn't care. Most of them were leaving in a day or two, and whether I told them the facts or not, the story would soon become myth. I swallowed my blood pressure pill with my tea, and with medicine and food in my belly I began to feel calm, if not happy.

I heard a helicopter come over the Abbey at around 3:00 and knew it was MacDonald's transport for the Kentuckians. I looked out my window and saw the big brown vehicle land on the road in front of the Abbey. The constable was there, giving directions, and I went out to talk with him. When the blades finally stopped, the sand settled down, and it was quiet enough for us to hear each other, he came over to me.

"This'll take us to Glasgow. They can catch a plane home from therrre."

"And Marilyn?"

"I'll turrrn herrr overrr to athorrrities there."

"How is she?"

"She's holdin' up."

"Good."

He pushed back his hat and scratched his head. "Y'know," he said, his eyes narrow, "it's fikkin odd."

"What is?"

"The way that woman confessed. No one everrr does that anymorrre. They've all learned frrrom the television prrrograms that if you keep quiet and neverrr admit anything, it's harrrd to convict ya. So therrre's no such thing as a confession, not here in the U.K."

"Confession is good for the soul," I said.

"What?"

"It relieves the burden of guilt," I explained. "People feel better when they come clean, even if it means punishment, especially if it means punishment. That's something the Church saw early on. Confession, it's part of the Church's genius. People like to confess."

"I guess. Still these days it's fikkin odd."

"Yes."

"In fact, all a life's fikkin odd."

"Yes."

The Kentuckians struggled out of Fellowship Hall, dragging their luggage. One by one they got into the helicopter. The Harrisons and the Joneses looked relieved and happy to be going home. Tom Edwards looked like his world had come to an end, and perhaps it had. Marilyn Jackson passed me and got aboard without acknowledging my presence. Wes Kelly and Jack Jackson came last. Wes shook my hand, looked embarrassed, and then embraced me.

"Thank you, Father," he said. "It's all a tragedy, but at least we know the truth. As the Scriptures say, the truth. . ."

"I know, Pastor, I know."

"Now I must go home, tell the story in full so people get it right, bury Beth, try to help Tom find his way, try to heal the wounds."

"It will be a big job," I said.

"Pray for me, Father," he said. "Ask God to help me."

"Well," I said. "God and I. . ." Then I let it drop. I knew he would never understand about God and me.

He smiled and climbed abroad the helicopter. The blades began to swirl, and gradually the noise increased. Only Jack Jackson remained. "You're going to stay with her in Glasgow?" I said.

"Yes," he said. "I'll find a place near where she is kept. I won't go home until she does."

"That may be a long time."

"Yes. Well, we have no children, and I'll encourage our parents to come here from time to time. Anyway, I'm here for the duration."

"How will you live? How will you pay your bills?"

"I'll check into teaching. Either at a school or private lessons. I'm pretty versatile. Voice, piano, a couple of horns and a couple of strings. I'll make out."

"You sure you want to do this?"

"I have to. It's my fault, mine and Beth's. She's paid her penalty, and it's a lot worse than mine. I have to make atonement. Maybe after a few years Marilyn will forgive me and we can live together again."

"All my best," I said.

He didn't shake my hand or embrace me. He just nodded and climbed aboard the helicopter.

MacDonald was the last to get on. "I told the Rrrreverrrend that they will ship Beth's body home within the week. That'll give him time t'be ready for it." He shook his head. "I still say," he mused, "life's fikkin odd."

I laughed. "I think you have something there, Constable."

He climbed aboard, gave the pilot a signal, and the blade picked up speed. Noise and sand started blasting me. I watched the helicopter and its load of Methodists rise toward heaven and then head south across the strait.

On my way back to my room:

"SO YOU DID IT AGAIN."

"Yes, I did it again. You know, I thought I was coming here to rest and think about things."

"WELL, YOU GOT TO THINK ABOUT THINGS, A LOT OF THINGS. ONE OUT OF TWO'S NOT BAD."

"It's not the kind of thinking I had in mind."

"BUT IT'S GOOD FOR YOU. YOU NEED TO KEEP YOUR MIND ACTIVE. IT STAVES OFF DEMENTIA."

"Thanks a lot."

"DON'T MENTION IT. BESIDES YOU HAVE TWO MORE WEEKS HERE. THAT'S PLENTY OF TIME TO REST AND VEGETATE."

"Thanks a lot."

"DON'T MENTION IT."

XII

Father Columba lived on Iona for many more years, died there at a ripe old age, and was buried in the cemetery of the original wooden Abbey, near the grave of Brother John. He was the ninth person to be interred there. His grave site was lost, along with those of the Scottish and Norwegian kings, during the destructive phase of the Reformation.

The longer he lived, and in years after his death, more and more miracles came to be associated with his name. The most dramatic of them was that he once waged hand to hand combat with Satan atop a mountain on Mull. This was a step forward from the one earlier attributed to him in which he and the Devil waged a verbal battle over the offer of world power. On Mull he was said to have fought Satan for three days and nights and finally defeated him, picked him up, and sent him skidding toward the sea, creating the ten miles long Loch Buie.

He was said to have healed so many illnesses that during his lifetime no disease dared come to the west of Scotland. This was said to explain the long life expectancy of people in the islands. Many of the miracles of the Bible, modified to match life in the Hebrides, were attributed to him. He was held to be a saint by people all over the British Isles long before he was officially proclaimed one by the Roman Catholic Church. Although he neither denied nor confirmed his belief that the Bishop of Rome was head of all the Church, he became a Catholic saint.

Long after his death, when the Benedictines took control of Iona, they built a stone Abbey on the holy ground where Columba's wooden structure had stood for six hundred years. Four hundred years after the erection of this solid structure, the example of King Henry VIII in England inspired Scottish Protestant Reformers to send the monks into exile, strip off the Abbey roof for its lead, and tell people of the islands to cart off wall stones to build their houses. Thus for another four hundred years the abbey lay in ruins, with cows grazing in the aisles, until the kindly local laird put up the money to reconstruct it and use it for interdenominational retreats. This was the building to which the twentieth century Father Columba, who was not and will likely never be a saint, made his retreat and identified who killed Beth Edwards.

Even during Saint Columba's life, Iona was an increasingly popular place of pilgrimage. Each week the number of people the blind man's sons ferried across the strait increased. Everyone who came wanted to talk with Columba, to tell him their concerns and their dreams and receive from him a message from God. At last, as his health declined, he placed the duties of running the Abbey, now numbering over fifty monks, into the hands of trusted assistants. At the same time he limited the number of visitors who came to the island and then gradually turned over the duties of meeting with them to carefully selected aids. One of the aids interviewed the pilgrims, sent each to a monk with the special talents of dealing with his or her concerns, and only in very rare occasions asked Columba if he would consent to take a special case.

One pilgrim who was brought to his attention in the last year of his life was a man who said he had a message from Brother Peter.

"Brother Peter?" Columba said when the aid brought him the message. The name stirred long buried memories. In all the years since Brother John's death on The Forest Isle, he had never given the name Peter to another monk. Even a young man whose name before he joined the Community was Peter and asked to keep it as his religious name was denied.

"No," Columba told him. "That name is reserved. It can never again be granted, not to anyone on Iona. "I shall call you Simon. That was Peter's name before Jesus named him Rock."

"Peter?" Columba repeated. "Did the man say how it was he came to know Brother Peter?"

"No, Master. He only said he knew him in Germania," the aid said.

"Germania? Then I don't. . ." He was about to deny the request for an interview, it couldn't be the same Peter, but then he thought perhaps a message from Peter in Germania made sense. Peter had been sent to convert the Saxons, and the Saxons had come to Britain from Germania. "Wait," he said. "Yes, all right, you may send him to me. I will see this man."

Columba was seated in his simple cell when the aid ushered the pilgrim through the door. The man was ragged, dirty, and thin, and he had obviously been on the road traveling for many weeks, perhaps months. He stood nervously waiting for Columba to speak.

"You have word for me from Brother Peter," Columba said with a soft voice, only slightly weakened by his age.

"I do, yes, Master," the man said.

"Then sit down. Here, in this chair."

The man trembled but took an uneasy seat.

"Where did you see Peter?"

"In the German lands, Master, near the Black Forest."

"Are you a German? You sound like a Scot."

"I am a Scot, Master. I was in Germania, passing through, on my way back from the Holy Land."

"You were in the Holy Land? Why did you go there?"

"I had. . .sinned, Master, sinned grievously; and my priest told me that the only way to win forgiveness was to make a pilgrimage to the Holy Places."

"You made it all the way there and back."

"I did, Master, by the grace of God."

"Yes, by God's grace, but you must also be intelligent to have survived all the dangers of that perilous journey."

The man blushed.

"You say you saw Peter."

"I went to see him in prison."

"Why was he in prison?"

"For preaching the Gospel to the heathen."

"German heathen."

"Yes, Father. He had been accused of vile crimes, none of which he had committed, he was guilty only of preaching the Gospel, but he was being held pending a trial."

"Did he say how he had come to be in the German lands?"

"He said a great man named Columba sent him to work among the Saxons in England, and he said he was successful, that he converted many more than the 666 that was his goal. He said he learned to preach in the Saxon tongue, and he preached in villages and fields, and people believed his message. He laughed when he told me that some of the Saxons identified him with the Apostle Peter and thought that he had known Jesus Christ personally. He said he did not deny this because it gave his message greater power and authority. He said that while he did not know Jesus Christ, he did know a man like Jesus Christ in holiness. He said this was Columba."

"He said I was like Jesus Christ?"

"Yes, Master, and when I asked him to tell me more about this Columba, he told me you lived—or he hoped you still lived—on Iona. I said I knew the place, I told him that I came from the western islands. He asked me to come and see you and tell you what had happened to him."

"Now you have, "Columba said. "How is he now? How was he when you left him?"

"Master, I am sorry, but he is dead."

"Dead."

"You may have heard about the barbaric system of justice the Germans practice. Well, he was put through it. He was submerged in a vat of water. They say if the water rejects an accused man, if he floats, he is guilty. Only if the water accepts him, in which case he often drowns, is he innocent. Brother Peter came to the surface, time and again, and he was proclaimed guilty."

"What was his sentence?"

"He was thrown off a high cliff."

Columba shuddered. Peter had spent his life trying to atone for Brother John's fall from the cliff on The Forest Isle, and in the end he had suffered the same fate. He thanked the pilgrim and gave him his own personal blessing.

"Now you go," he told the man, "and you tell Brother Peter's story, the story of a blessed martyr, to as many people as will listen. He will continue to serve God through your words."

The man promised to do so, and Columba walked with him to the door leading out of the Abbey. "Go in peace," he told the man, even though he knew that if the man did indeed tell Peter's story he would never know peace.

The man looked back once, from some distance, and he could see that Columba was weeping.

XIII

t dinner that night I finally got a full meal, my first for awhile. The other two tables were full, so I ate alone at the table vacated by the Kentuckians, which was fine, I needed the solitude. Other retreatants seemed to understand this. Another couple of days and everyone then in the dining room would be gone, to be replaced by new arrivals, and I would be the only one remaining from my first hectic week. Unless the staff told them about the murder and my role in solving the crime, I could spend the next two weeks in more or less anonymity.

It did cross my mind and the thought made me shudder that one of these would hear the story, or part of it, before he left and at some future date call on me to help solve another murder mystery the way Wes Kelly had done. I looked across at the other tables, searching for the face of that possible someone, but they all looked pretty blank to me. Blank faces, a good sign.

I went to bed early, hoping to sleep through the night, but about two in the morning someone knocked at my door. I roused and came partially awake, and the first thing that passed through my mind was that there had been another killing. I got up, stumbled three steps, and opened the door with trepidation. A stranger was standing there.

"Sorry to botherrr you, sirrr, but I'm the night attendant; and you have a telephone cool," the man said.

"I do?"

"Yes sirrr. The telephone is in the office downstairrrs. I wouldn't have wakened you, but the man said it was imporrrtant that you come. He insisted."

"All right," I said, pulling on my robe. "Lead the way."

I followed the man down the hallway, down the stairs, and into the office. He pointed toward the phone receiver lying face up on the table and left me alone, closing the door behind him. I picked it up.

"Yes? This is Father Columba," I said cautiously.

"Columba? That you?" It was Father Abbot.

"Yes, it is, Abbot. In the middle of the night."

"What?" He went into a coughing fit. Finally recovering, he went on. "Oh yes, I'd forgotten about the difference in time. It's still evening here."

"It would be," I said with some sarcasm.

I found it hard to believe he had forgotten about the time difference. He had studied in Rome as a young man and then lived in Asia for several years, and surely he had called home during those times and knew there were twenty four time zones. Surely he knew that Europe is several hours ahead of Pennsylvania.

"How are you?" he said without any apology. "I was just calling to see how your first week went?"

"Well, let's just say it has been. . .interesting."

"Have you felt the spirit of Saint Columba?"

"Not unless we learn that Columba solved murder mysteries."

"What? Don't tell me, you've had another one?"

"Yes."

"Yes? Really? They seem to follow you."

"You could say that."

"What was this one about?" He coughed again but was able to restrict this one to a quick couple of hacks.

"I was able to help a group of Methodists sort out a death in their family."

"What? You're cutting out on me."

"I was able. . ."

"What? Say it again."

"Never mind," I said. I thought better of trying to tell him the story in a transatlantic call. "I'll tell you about it when I get home."

"You say you're anxious to get home?"

"Uh, yes, Father."

"Be it ever so humble, no place like it, eh?"

"No.

"You have another couple of weeks there, right?"

"Yes."

"Well, hang loose. There could be more adventures waiting."

"Oh joy."

"Actually I may have another assignment for you after that. No need for you to hurry back. Things here are still not completely settled. Some people are still not happy about your theology."

"I'll wait for further instructions."

"Have you done any thinking? You know, that opinion you have, about God, I mean? Have you given. . ." Another coughing fit. This one went on and on, and I thought he might have to terminate the conversation; but he persevered, as always, and at last he went on with his interrogation, his voice strained from the exertion. "Any changes in your opinion of the Divine?"

"No, Father," I said with a sigh. "Same old same old."

"Still my favorite heretic?" He laughed.

"I am *not* a heretic," I said with some heat, and he stopped laughing.

"No. Of course not," he said. "But you still find God something of, shall we say, a mixed blessing?"

"Yes, Father, I do. A mixed blessing indeed."

"Hmmmm," he said.

"As I do man. What I've seen this weeks confirms it. Man can be good, man can be bad. Like God, he's a mixed blessing." I thought about it. "After all, it's to be expected. The Bible says that man is made in the image of God."

"I'm not sure that's what the Scripture means, Columba."

"Maybe it is. Maybe that's why man is a mystery. He's so much like God," the greatest of mysteries."

"Columba. . ."

"It's late, Father Abbot."

"What? Oh. Oh yes. You need to get back to sleep. Well, keep your chin up. Remember. . ." The cough came again. ". . .as our good Bishop Sheen says so aptly, 'Life is Worth Living.'"

"Maybe so, Father," I yawned. I was sleepy, and when I am sleepy I sometimes get careless. I felt an urge to shock. "By the way, I have made the acquaintance of a Scottish theologian this week, and he said something you might put alongside 'Life is Worth Living.' He says, 'Life can be fikkin odd.'"

"What? What was that last part? You're cutting out again."

"It's just as well, Father, it's just as well." I hung up.

Back in my room, in the darkness, I heard the familiar voice.

"ABOUT WHAT CONSTABLE MACDONALD SAID. . ."

"Shhh," I said. "Let me sleep."

About the Author

J ames Baker developed his passion for history and religion while in high school, during his days as a Bulldog. He is a graduate of Baylor and Florida State Universities and has for many years taught at Western Kentucky University. Throughout his career he has been a prolific writer, authoring 22 books and over 60 articles. His articles have appeared in such places as *Christian Century, Commonweal, The Chronicle of Higher Education*, and *The American Benedictine Review*. His creative talents and his unique points of view

and insights have also made him a highly sought after speaker. He has delivered addresses and papers in the United States, Italy, Korea, Taiwan, China, and other Asian countries. He often appears in a one person show-presentation of industrialist-philanthropist Andrew Carnegie. In addition to his teaching duties, James directs the Canadian Parliamentary Internship Program.

Made in the USA
Charleston, SC
07 August 2014